Dedication

I want to dedicate this book to my husband, Alan and my two children, Kiera and Rhys. Thank you for believing in me and allowing me the time to do this!

I love you all and I hope I've made you proud!

1 Kammie

Today I'm going to a wedding! My best friend's wedding! I can't wait!

Tasha has been through a lot in the last year or so, she deserves to be happy. Her husband, Felix, abused her after they got married and she never told me - I was hurt when I found out and realised she hadn't spoken to me about it, but that hurt didn't last long because she needed me and I was there for her when she did.

I can't believe she came out of that relationship and met the man of her dreams, the man who has made her happy and today will be making her his and he will protect her for the rest of her life. Caleb is wonderful and I'm so happy for them both.

I'm getting dressed when my boyfriend, Luca walks in to see how I'm getting on. "Wow Kammie you look so beautiful," he says as he comes over and stands behind me looking into the mirror. He leans down and kisses me on the nape of my neck, while sliding the zip up on my dress. "It's going to be a good day today, I can feel it," he says smiling at me in the mirror.

I turn to face him and say "Luca every day is a good day when I'm with you," and I stand on my tip toes and kiss him on the lips. It's always hard to only give him a quick kiss because I want to consume him, I need him, I love him.

He smacks me on the bum and I squeal and then we both start laughing. "I know today will be hard on you Luca, I'm here if you find it difficult, you know that don't you?" I look deep into his eyes, searching for his soul.

"I know Kammie, I'll be fine. I like Caleb a lot and I know how happy he makes Tasha and that's what matters! For her to get her happy ending, she deserves it so much!" He takes a deep breath and then smiles at me, he takes me and pulls me into a hug. "I love you Kammie, I really do, I can't believe that you're mine."

"Ditto Luca, ditto!" We continue hugging for a couple of minutes and then I slowly pull away. "Come on you'll ruin my hair and makeup, we need to get a move on," he smiles and then we get our things together and drive to Tasha and Caleb's house.

They are having the wedding at the beach house, it's beautiful and I've helped Tasha to make sure everything is arranged perfectly. Tasha didn't really have much input into her first wedding to Felix, so she has gone for something she always wanted, a dream wedding.

We arrive at the house and everyone is excited and waiting for Tasha. We seek out Caleb and when we find him he is really nervous! I'm surprised, he is such a confident man and him and Tasha have an amazing bond. They are true soul mates, he knows when she's hurting and he knows just how to help her. He always has done, ever since the moment they first met.

"Are you ok Caleb, what's the matter?" I ask because he looks a bit pale.

"I'm fine, well apart from being nervous," he laughs slightly. "What if she doesn't want to go through with it? What's if she's decided she doesn't want to marry me anymore?"

I can't believe I'm hearing this, it's just not like him. "Caleb, calm down, you know how she feels about you. Concentrate on making sure everything is going right down here." I rub his arm. "Will I go and check on her and make sure she is ok? Will that make you feel better?"

He nods "Yeah it would. Would you do that for me?" he smiles and hugs me.

"I'll be right back Luca, Caleb I'll come and find you ok!"

He smiles his beautiful smile at me and I turn and walk towards the stairs to go up and find Tasha.

Luca

I stand there and watch Kammie walk away from me and go up the stairs to her best friend. I feel a little bit emotional, she was right when she said that it was going to be a hard day, but I'm happy for Tasha, she deserves her happy ending.

You see just over a year ago Tasha married my best friend in the world, Felix. It was such a beautiful day and they were both so happy, what none of us realised was that Felix was like a ticking time bomb and he started to abuse Tasha in their own home and she didn't tell any of us. That's what really hurts, that she didn't tell me or Kammie, but what hurts more is that my best friend, who I've known for ever, didn't come to me and ask for help.

I know I can't help him now, but I would have done anything to help. When I first found out something was wrong I spoke to Tasha and she begged me not to say anything to Felix, she pleaded with me. I didn't want to make things worse and she promised me it wouldn't happen again. I did speak to Felix and asked him what was wrong with him and why he had changed. He just said that he loved Tasha and he would do anything to keep her safe. Little did I know he was the one she needed keeping safe from.

I remember the night I got the call from Felix to tell me to get over to the house, he had hurt Tasha and he had locked her in the bathroom to stop him from hurting her more. It was like he was battling with himself, I rushed over there and there was blood everywhere, he had smashed the room up and then he had slit his wrists. My initial reaction was one of shock because Felix was a strong man, he was confident, good looking and he loved Tasha more than life itself. I left Tasha in the bathroom until I knew Felix was in the ambulance, I was worried about opening the door, I didn't know what he had done to her. Luckily Kammie was with me when I got the phone call and she came with me, I told her to avert her eyes because she didn't need to see what Felix had done. She sat at the bathroom door talking to Tasha, trying to keep her calm.

Felix ended up staying in hospital for a couple of weeks, he had psychiatric treatment and they finally agreed to let him go home. I had said I would stay with him, but he didn't want me to. If only I had stayed then I wouldn't have lost my best friend. You see Felix invited Tasha over to collect her stuff, he knew they shouldn't be together anymore, and after he spoke to her he hung himself and did it so that Tasha would find him. I can't believe he was so selfish to do that to that poor beautiful woman.

I blame myself for what happened to Felix, I knew he was sick and I knew I should've stayed with him, but I allowed him to stop me.

Anyway, today Tasha gets her happy ending and I intend to enjoy every minute of it because I love her so much and she didn't deserve what that bastard did to her.

Caleb is looking worried as Kammie is taking quite a while. "Hey mate, she'll be fine, stop worrying, you two are meant to be together, everyone knows that!" I smile at him and slap him on the shoulder the way guys do.

"I know we are but until I see her walking down the aisle to me, I'm going to panic, I've never felt so nervous about anything before Luca" he laughs.

Caleb is a great guy and has become a close friend, ironically. He was the guy that Tasha talked to throughout her problems with Felix, he was her rock. Their relationship blossomed quite quickly after Felix died, but when they are together it is like they are one person.

"Look here's Kammie now, Caleb, she's smiling so that has to be good right" I smile at him, he turns to look at Kammie. Kammie who has been my rock and who is so beautiful it still makes me catch my breath when I look at her. I smile at her "Well ..... " I say with my eyebrows raised.

She smiles at Caleb "Caleb stop worrying, she said to tell you that she can't wait to be Mrs Hunt and she will see you in her most favourite spot in the world in a few minutes" Caleb starts to smile and you can see him physically relax.

I'm happy that he has been reassured, he gives Kammie a kiss on the cheek and then says "Right then let's get everyone sat outside and then we can get married." He walks off and starts asking people to move outside and take their places. I take Kammie's hand and we move out onto the balcony for the ceremony.

2 Kammie

As I watch Tasha walk down the aisle towards Caleb and see the radiance in her face, I'm happy, truly happy. She deserves this, she deserves Caleb and she deserves a good life. I turn to look at Luca and I can't believe he's mine, he is an amazing person, so thoughtful and so hot in bed. I blush slightly thinking of the things we got up to last night, I thought I was an experienced woman but he certainly opened my eyes to sex and I love every minute of it.

He turns and smiles at me "What are you thinking about that put that blush and smile on your face?"

"I was thinking about last night and how

amazing it was, you never cease to amaze me Luca," I blush.

He laughs "It takes two baby to make it perfect" he leans down and kisses me.

He holds my hand throughout the whole ceremony and looks at me regularly, I really do love him and can't quite believe he's mine. Through all of the ups and downs of the last year, something fantastic came out of it all: mine and Lucas's love for each other. He goes and gets me a drink and I look around to find Tasha and give her a hug.

I find her holding Caleb's hand, she looks like she doesn't want to let go. This wedding is so different to her last one with Felix, she organised everything and loved every minute of it, everything and everyone here today is her doing.

"Hey bitch, how's your day going?" I say hugging her and smiling.

She laughs "Oh Kammie I'm having a great day, everyone seems so happy" I can see tears forming in her eyes, I know she's feeling emotional today and I know why!

"Why wouldn't we all be happy Tasha, it's a beautiful day and you and Caleb are so happy and that makes us all happy. Me and

Luca are going to mingle before dinner, I can't wait for the speeches" I say winking at her. What I really mean is I can't wait until she gives her present to Caleb - he is going to be beside himself. I wink at her again and then I take Luca's arm and walk away.

"You know she went to the grave on the way here" I say rubbing his hand.

"No I didn't realise that, was she ok?" he asks, I can see he is in shock.

"Yes she wanted to go and say goodbye properly and she said thank you to him for setting her free!" We've walked back outside to the decking and are now looking out to the sea.

"Wow it's amazing she's forgiven him and taken the positive side through all this. She hasn't let it defeat her," he stares at the sea for a few minutes. "You know it still hurts Kammie, I miss him so much even after everything he did to Tasha" he looks so sad.

"I know you do Luca, I'm here for you though, you know you can tell me everything" I say kissing him.

He pulls me in close to him and puts one arm around me keeping me close to him. The other hand holds me at the nape of my neck, very gently pulling my hair so that I tip my face up to him. I love when he does that, he applies just the right amount of pressure. "I know you are baby and I am so thankful you are. I don't know how we managed to find each other during such a traumatic time. I love you Kammie. Don't ever leave me. I need you." He slams his mouth down onto mine with such emotion that I can feel his heart beating through his kiss.

I love him so much, when I think back over the last couple of years and how we would socialise and be friends and want more but never taking it further, how did we get to this situation?

3 Luca

Two years ago!

"Come on Felix, come out tonight, I know you met someone but don't give up your freedom yet man!" I'm frustrated with Felix he always falls head over heels with someone straight away, then he gets serious and the girls start backing off. He goes on mad benders and gets drunk and stupid, I'm trying to stop this cycle from happening this time. The girl he met Natasha, is lovely, she is beautiful and if it wasn't for Felix being my best friend, I would be in there like a shot. She looks really shy but I bet she's hot in bed. Obviously, I don't say this to Felix, he would murder me, he gets possessive over his girlfriends, he knows I won't try anything on with them, it's an unwritten rule. However, he thinks they might fancy me so he always tried to keep them away from me as long as possible.

He agrees to come out tonight as long as Tasha, as he calls her, can comeout too. "Of course she can mate, does she have any friends? Get her to bring some of them out too" I laugh.

He laughs back at me "I'll see what I can do, but I don't think her friends are into your kind of shit Luca."

"What the fuck mate?" I laugh "My kind of shit keeps me getting the girls every week Felix."

"Yeah but you don't hold onto them Luca, when are you going to settle down?" he asks me.

"Look Felix, I don't need to settle down yet, I'm enjoying myself and I like having different women every week, it makes my life interesting and I can wait until I find the right woman before I need to calm myself down." I'm laughing now because I sound so abnoxious. "See what you can do, we'll meet you in The Angel Pub and then go to Jesters after that"

Felix agrees and hangs up the phone, it's early on Saturday morning and I have to be in work in 20 minutes, I'm already up and dressed in my work gear: basketball shorts and skin tight t-shirt, I work in a gym and today I run a couple of classes for women. I always make sure I look my best when I know it's the women's class, you never know where your next bit of fun will come along.

I go to work and the classes are strenuous, they make you sweat, then again I did show Bethany how we work out in the store cupboard, the only thing is she makes too much noise to be shagging her at work. I won't be doing that again. I laugh to myself.

My last class today is a mixed spinning class, it is torturous. I really work them hard, but they love it. We have a good laugh even though it's tough. They're a great group. When we're finished, I grab my bag and drive home.

I make myself some dinner, I love cooking, but I never cook for any women, they'd expect more than I'm willing to give them. After dinner I shower, change and generally spruce myself up. I like to make sure my clothes, hair and everything is matching and perfect. It works for me so why not!

I've arranged to meet Glenn, my friend from school, at 9pm in The Angel Pub, so I take the bus into town, there are a lot of people already out and already drunk. The women wear very little clothes so you don't need to leave anything up to the imagination. I always look around to see who I fancy next, it's great fun, Glenn loves coming out with me because he always ends up with a woman because they usually come out in pairs.

I get off the bus and walk to the pub, I see Glenn at the bar ordering the drinks, he must have just arrived. I walk over to him "Hey Glenn mate, how's things? Any news?" I slap him on the shoulder, he turns and smiles at me.

"You're looking good tonight Luca, what do you reckon our chances are?" he says looking around the pub.

I take a quick look around myself and then I say "Good mate, good," we both crack up laughing. We have a couple of drinks here and eye up all the lovely ladies when we see Felix walking in with two beautiful girls. "Oh my god look at Felix" I say to Glenn "I wonder who that is with Tasha, she is stunning. Hands off she's mine" I laugh, but meaning the warning.

Glenn laughs at me and then Felix is in front of us, "Hey guys, you both know Tasha and this is her best friend Kammie" he looks at me with a warning in his eyes. "What do you two girls want to drink?" he asks them. They tell him and then he starts walking to the bar "Don't you dare Luca, don't even attempt it. If you sleep with her once and then dump her it would make it very awkward, I'm falling for Tasha big time and I need you guys to be friends."

"Ok Felix, I won't go there, but if you and Tasha split up, I'm moving in on Kammie, she is gorgeous," I say feeling slightly disappointed. I turn to look at the two girls and see Kammie laughing with Glenn, something stirs in my stomach, it's a strange feeling and something I've never felt before.

I help Felix back with the drinks and when I hand Kammie her drink I hold onto it for slightly too long because I'm touching her hand, she looks up at me through her lashes. "Are you going to hold onto that all night?" she says with the silkiest voice I've ever heard, so much so I feel a tingling in my cock. Wow she is trouble and I'd better stay well clear!

"Sorry I don't know what's wrong with

me. Are you ready to party and have a good night?" I ask, I'm staring into her eyes and I feel like I'm going to drown in them, this is very strange for me I never feel like this, I shake my head to bring myself back to reality.

"Well I wasn't sure about coming out tonight with some of Felix's friends, he's a really nice guy but I like to party and have fun and he's a bit serious for me, if you know what I mean!" She says looking up at me with a smile on her face. She is flirting with me, I think I've met my match here, I can feel the blood pumping around my veins, I can hear my heart beating faster, it's like time is slowing down.

I look down at her, straight into her eyes, they are an amazing grey colour, they are so unusual "Oh I know what you mean alright. Come on then let's get this party started," I say turning to the others, I need to put some distance between us because I don't like the way my body reacts to her, well that a lie, I like it a lot how it reacts.

"Come on let's go to Jesters guys, let's get dancing and drinking." We all finish our drinks and then walk out of the pub to Jesters, Kammie walks with Tasha and Felix hangs back with us "Mate, I don't know if I can leave her alone tonight, she was practically begging me in there, I know I promised, but can I get a one night pass, please?"

Felix laughs really loud "Ha ha are you getting pussy whipped? That is really funny."

"No, she's just everything I look for and more, she has that bit of a sparkle in her eyes, I reckon she would be a match for me in the bedroom department and I like the idea of that." I smile just thinking of everything we could get up to.

"No Luca, I can't lose Tasha because of you and your dick" he says seriously, he holds out his hand to shake mine, I reluctantly shake it, but I don't smile about it.

All of a sudden I don't feel like partying, but I'm here now I might as well make the most of it.

4 Kammie

I don't know what hit me when I saw Luca, he is so sexy, Mr Perfection in all its glory and I felt the attraction between us, I'm quite excited about it, I can feel myself getting wet between my legs, so much so I have to cross them. Tasha comes up to me in the queue for Jesters and says to me "Kammie, I know you're attracted to Luca it's really obvious, but I need you to stay well away, he is a player and he never takes the same woman home twice, a bit like you really. I don't want you to be hurt by him and then not come out with us again, me and Felix are getting serious and I don't want anything to ruin it just for a night of sex. Do you know what I'm saying?" I nod because I know what she means, even though I don't like it.

"There's no harm in flirting though - right?" I say grinning at her. She looks at me and then doubles over with laughter, thank god I lightened the situation.

The night is a roaring success, I flirt with Luca most of the night, but I'm guessing we both know we can't go home with each other and so about an hour from the end of the club, me and Tasha go off dancing. I'm so horny I need to find a man to take me home and give me exactly what I'm craving right now.

When we're on the dance floor I spot a guy watching me, he is hot and looks like just the man to "scratch my itch", I make sure we move closer to him while we are dancing. I do my sexy moves which show off my body and then when I see him watching me, I wink at him.

He comes over and asks do we want a drink, I see Tasha look over to Felix, who doesn't look too happy, then she says "I have to go back to Felix, Kammie will you be ok?"

I nod my head and tell her "I'll ring you when I get home safe and sound, talk to you in the morning bitch," that's my nickname for her because it is the total opposite of what she is. I watch her walk off and then I turn to face the guy "Yeah I'll have a drink" I say linking his arm and pushing him towards the bar. I am happy because I am so going to get laid tonight.

Luca

I see Tasha and Kammie dancing, wow is all I can think. Felix is so lucky and so is whoever goes home with Kammie. I want it to be me so bad, but I know I have to respect Felix especially when he's getting serious with Tasha.

Tasha comes walking over to us "I need a drink, I'm wrecked after all that dancing" Felix passes her her drink.

"Where's Kammie?" I ask looking behind Tasha.

"She picked up a guy, she's over at the other bar getting a drink" she says in between gulps of her drink.

I feel disappointed; I was enjoying flirting with her and thought she felt the same, obviously not. Well I'm not going to waste my time waiting for her to come back, so I turn to Glenn and say "Come on mate it's near the end of the night. I think I've wasted too much time on something that isn't going to happen." I grab hold of his arm and pull him to stand at the side of the dance floor to see who we are going to be taking home tonight.

I'm looking around the dance floor and I see Bethany from my class looking at me smiling, I know I said I don't revisit the same girl but I'm horny and just need sex. She might take my mind off Kammie. I start to walk over to her when I see Kammie out of the corner of eye, she looks like she is trying to pull away from the guy who was buying her a drink, she looks really angry, I can't ignore her so I walk over to them. I slide my arm around her waist and say "There you are baby, I wondered where you went" I take the opportunity to kiss her on the cheek, she looks up at me and once again I feel the intensity of her gaze on my dick. "Are you ok? Is this guy bothering you baby?"

She looks at me and smiles, "No he was just buying me a drink, but now you're back I'm good. I wondered where you went I thought you'd left me" she giggles a little, god I love that noise. I think that's my new favourite thing in the world, it has the power to turn me on in an instant.

"I'd never leave you baby, come on let's get out of here, don't forget to thank the man for the drink" I say laughing at her. She says thanks him and then puts her arm around my waist and we walk away. When we are far enough away she drops her arm and I ask her "Are you ok?"

"Yeah thank you for rescuing me there, he wanted me to pick another girl and have a threesome, I wasn't in the mood for that so he got mad when I said that to him," she looks at me and I'm trying not to start laughing, what a girl! "Thanks again Luca" she leans up and kisses me on the cheek, it takes everything in my power not to move so that I can kiss her properly, she feels like a firework waiting to go off.

"Come on Kammie let's get out of here" I say taking her hand and pulling her out into the street. "Do you fancy going for something to eat, there's a great coffee shop down the road here?" I ask with trepidation because I really don't want her to say no.

"Yeah come on it's too early to finish for the night" she says smiling at me.

I still have hold of her hand so we walk side by side to the coffee shop. We find a booth at the back and I order two americano's and a slice of Apple pie, my favourite, but I pick up 2 spoons, we can share!

When I bring them back to the table she looks at me like she's going to eat me and I smile. It's only then I realise she's looking at the apple pie. What is this girl doing to me?

"Luca I can't believe you bought apple pie, that's my favourite, are we sharing?" she says looking at the spoons.

"Yes, I love apple pie and I can think of no one better to share my pie with tonight" I smile.

We sit and talk for over an hour and then we are asked to leave because they want to close the coffee shop. We stand and I place my hand on the lower part of her back, she turns to look at me and then smiles. I just want to run my hands all over her body, she is driving me insane.

"Will you walk me to the taxi rank, please?" She obviously feels the same and doesn't want the night to end. Damn Felix and Tasha!

"Of course I will Kammie, what kind of guy would I be if I didn't make sure you got home safely, I'm going to jump in the cab with you and then it can take me to my place after we drop you off." I take her hand and we walk past 3 taxi ranks before we stop.

We get into the car, still holding hands when all of sudden she says to me "Can I ask you a question Luca? I want you to be honest with me."

"Of course you can and of course I will" I say not knowing what's coming next.

"Do you fancy me?" She says looking at the floor, gone is the confident woman who can get any man she wants. This Kammie turns me on even more than the other Kammie did and I didn't think that was possible.

"Kammie, you are the most beautiful creature that I have ever seen. Yes I do fancy you, why?" I ask.

"I just wondered because I fancy you, but ..." She pauses, here it comes the brush off.

"But? ..." I ask

"But I'm guessing you got the same talk from Felix that I got from Tasha" she says looking sad.

I start laughing "Yeah I did! The one about it being awkward because we usually just sleep with someone and move on. Is that the one?"

She starts laughing too "Yep that's the one. Guess our reputations precede us Luca" she leans her head back on the seat and closes her eyes, she looks tired.

"What are we going to do then Kammie, I want you so badly, I'm not sure I can just leave you at your door tonight, I don't want tonight to end" I move closer to her and rest my head on the back of the seat too.

"Me neither Luca, you can come and stay the night but I don't think we should do anything, I like you too much to only do it once." She laughs. "Assuming you'd want to do it more than once" she's getting flustered now, she's so cute when she blushes.

"I'd like that a lot Kammie, we can just talk and sleep, I promise to behave." I say smiling at her.

We pull up to her house and she gets out, I follow after paying the taxi. I take her hand and she pulls me into her house. It's lovely inside, she has a flair for decorating. We go into the kitchen and she opens a bottle of wine, then she tells me to follow her and we go upstairs to the bedroom. She goes into the bathroom and gets undressed and puts her pj's on, now I don't know why she bothers to wear them because I can see everything and my cock is not behaving itself.

I take my trousers and shirt off and get into bed. I think this will be the first time ever that I've slept with a girl and not had sex with her. It's going to be a long night!

She slides in next to me and I give her the glass of wine I just poured for her. She starts giggling, it is really an amazing sound. My dick is twitching in my pants, I might need to take a cold shower but I don't want to leave her.

We laugh and drink for about an hour then I can see she's getting tired. "Come on Kammie I know you're tired, let's go to sleep" I take her empty glass and put it on the bedside table. I turn out the light and slide down the bed under the covers. "Can I cuddle you Kammie? I promise to behave" I ask, it's silent for a while. "It's ok if you don't want to I just thought I'd ask, I'd love to hold you all night" I say slightly disappointed.

I go to turn over, but I feel her hand on my arm "Luca I want that so much, I just don't know if I can behave myself" she giggles, "please hold me Luca I'll behave too" she rolls onto her side and I do to, then I put my arm around her waist and gently pull her back towards me.

"Ok Kammie but don't complain if I start to feel horny, you really are beautiful, but I promise that I will behave" I laugh as she wiggles her bum until she's touching my body. I can hear her breathing start to slow down, I take a few minutes to breathe in her scent and then I feel myself drifting off to sleep. Heaven!

5 Kammie

As I'm waking up I can feel a strong arm around my waist, pulling me back so that I can't move. I start to panic, I don't cuddle any of the men I bring home because I don't want to see them again. I hear a groan and look over my shoulder and there he is, beautiful and I think I must be dreaming. He opens one eye and looks at me and smiles "Morning gorgeous did you sleep well?" I turn back away and snuggle back into him, it just feels so natural.

"Morning Luca, I slept well considering I was kept in the same place all night" I laugh.

He laughs back "Well I didn't want you to get away, I wanted to take as much as I could without taking you" he leans forward and kisses me on the shoulder. "Best night sleep ever!"

"Mmmm this not having sex is actually quite fun" I say in between giggles.

I hear him moan "God Kammie do you know how much you turn me on when you do that?" He puts his hand on the bottom of my stomach and pulls me back all the way so I can feel his erection.

"Luca please don't, it's torture enough and I really need to get out of bed, come on let's be good and have breakfast." I try to pull away but he won't let me go.

"Can't we lay in bed a while longer and just talk, please Kammie I want to know more about you. You fascinate me" he kisses my shoulder again, I wish he would stop that, it tingles all the way down to my pussy.

"OK but stop sticking your cock in between my ass cheeks Luca it's distracting." I say wriggling my bum on his cock.

"Ha ha" he's laughing so much I can feel my whole body shaking. We stay like that for a couple of hours laughing and talking then my phone rings, it's Tasha.

"Shh Luca, it's Tasha I don't want her to know we spent the night together." I kiss him quickly on the cheek because I don't want to upset him.

"Hey Tasha sorry couldn't find my phone. How are you today?" I ask.

"I'm good, my head isn't too bad considering. Where did you disappear to? I looked for you but you'd gone. Was everything ok?"

"Yeah I had a bit of hassle with that guy who bought me a drink so I decided to leave I'd had enough to drink anyway" I say smiling at Luca.

"So," she says "What did you think of Luca? Didn't I tell you he was gorgeous" I'm blushing because I know he can hear Tasha and he's looking at me as if to say "Yeah what did you think of me?"

"Yeah he is gorgeous but he knows it too" I laugh sticking my tongue out at him.

She laughs too "I know but you two looked like you were having loads of fun."

"Yeah we were having fun, I don't know why I had to agree to staying away from him Tasha he is just my type - fun, not serious but I bet he's shit in bed though." I laugh, Luca scowls at me and has sat up in the bed, oh oh I think I'm in trouble.

"That's not what I heard Kammie, I

heard he's an animal between the sheets" she is rolling around laughing.

"Tasha I really have to go, there's someone at my door, sorry bitch I'll ring you later. Love you. Bye"

I hang up and turn to face Luca and before I can say anything he pounces on me and pins my arms at the side of my head, he's straddled my waist. "Don't move Kammie I am seconds from tying you to this bed and ignoring Felix and Tasha. You are such a tease and it just makes me want you more, I want to spank you because you're being so naughty" he looks down at me and loosens his grip on my arms. I look him up and down and I can see his cock through his boxers because they are skin tight. I gasp, it looks huge, I know it felt huge but looking at it like that, I try to close my legs because I can feel I'm getting wet.

I slowly raise my eyes to look at him and before I know it he crashes his mouth down on mine. He is laying on top of me now and I can feel all of him, I want him so badly. I kiss him back with as much passion as he is giving me. All of a sudden he pulls back, "I'm sorry Kammie I couldn't help myself. I have to go, I don't think I can keep my hands off you." He gets up from the bed, grabs his clothes and walks into the bathroom. I sit there with my arms around my bent legs and my head resting on my knees, it's hard not to cry. I suppose this is what Tasha was talking about, the awkwardness!

Luca

I stay in the bathroom as long as I can, I take a cold shower and even that's not enough. Damn she is so hot and my body is still reacting to her, even though I heard her go downstairs. Shit! What am I going to do? I don't want to leave her, but we both know we can't start anything either. We both like to play the field too much and aren't ready to settle down, it would only be awkward if something went wrong, it's awkward now and we didn't even have sex.

OK Luca, man up and go down and make sure she knows how special she is. I finish getting dressed and then go downstairs into the kitchen where I can smell the coffee. "Hey" I say, I need to get a new line I think. "Is there a cup for me or did you want me to leave?" I ask.

"Here's a cup" she says handing it to me "knock yourself out" she smiles.

I walk over and make a cup and then I walk over to her, she is leaning up against the counter facing me, I put my cup on one side of her, then I rest my other hand on the other side of her, boxing her in. She slowly raises her eyes up to mine and I can see the sparkle in her eye once again. "I'm sorry Kammie, I was being a dick, I could have handled it better, it's just you do things to me that I don't understand baby" I'm leaning forward and I pull her gorgeous body into mine and I whisper in her ear "You deserve more than me Kammie, I'm not good enough for you."

She puts her arms around me and I can hear the catch in her breath "It would have been fun figuring that out though Luca" I don't know what to say, so I just hug her tighter.

I pull away and her head is looking at the floor, I put my finger under her chin and slowly raise it up. "Come on let's go in the lounge and watch a stupid film or something. Something that'll make us laugh." I don't want to go home, I'm not ready. She smiles and the whole of her face lights up including her eyes. She takes my hand and leads me to the couch, where I sit. We spend the next four hours watching silly comedies, both of us laughing; I laugh so hard my ribs hurt.

"I need to go home now Kammie, I desperately need to get out of these clothes" I say.

"Yeah I didn't want to tell you, but you smell" she starts laughing really hard, I push her down on the couch and lean above her.

"One day you are going to be in so much trouble I won't care what Tasha and Felix say." I lean down and kiss her soft wet lips very gently, then I lean back and pull her back up to sitting again.

"I can't wait" she says quietly but I hear her.

"So what are we going to do going forward baby? I've had more fun last night and today than I've ever had. I like our camaraderie and I like you a lot." Did those words just come out of my mouth? I'm turning into a sap. "I think we can be really good friends Kammie, I really like you, you're a fun person to be around" I know it's a bit cliché and I've never had a "girl" friend but I want her in my life.

"I've had fun too Luca, I know we can be good friends too, but don't expect me to stop chancing my arm and lead you on" she laughs. We are all good.

"Give me your number so I can ring you and check up on you, then if you ever need anything baby I'm here. OK?" I say getting my phone out.

She gives me her number and I ring it just to make sure it's hers, she smiles and looks at me "Did you really think I would give you a different number?"

"No but I just wanted to make sure" I say smiling back. She walks me to her door and I can't resist myself I lean forward and give her a kiss, she responds. After a minute we pull apart and I lean my forehead against hers "I really enjoyed last night and today, we must do it again sometime." She smiles back at me and then I turn to go through the door "See you Kammie, don't forget it you need anything I'm here ok."

"See you Luca, I won't forget thanks" she waves at me and then she closes her front door. She's gone just like that! Wow what happened last night? It all seems like a dream.

I walk home and it takes about an hour, then I put my gym stuff on and drive to work, I'm not working but I need to get rid of my pent up frustration. While I'm working out I can see Bethany smiling at me, to think I nearly took her home last night instead of spending the time with Kammie. Fate intervened so I think it's trying to tell me something. Bethany makes her way over to me "Hey Luc" it doesn't matter how many times I tell her my name is Luca she still feels she can shorten it.

"Hi Beth how are you, I saw you last night in Jesters." I smile back, she is a customer after all.

"Yeah I thought you were coming over to me and then you veered off in another direction." I think she's pouting!

"I saw a friend who needed rescuing" I said. I'm not apologising.

"Did you want something last night or even today Luc?" She says touching my arm. Oh my god she wants a repeat of yesterday, even if I wanted to, I couldn't because I have Kammie on my mind and I wouldn't do that to her after only a couple of hours. Did I just think that? I'm losing my playboy status here, but I still decline.

"No I was just coming over to say hi.

Now if you can excuse me Beth I have to finish my work out because I have to meet someone tonight." I know I'm being mean but I don't want her near me today.

"Oh, of course you're busy another time Luc" she says leaning in for a kiss. I move away just in time so that she doesn't makes contact.

I look at her turning on her heels and walking away, I let out the breath I was holding. Thank god I got rid of her, now let's get Kammie out of my mind. I pound the treadmill and then when I'm finished I shower and go home and get into bed.

I have a hard on and can't stop thinking of Kammie, so I whip my cock out and start stroking it, it's already hard but it gets harder and it's so hot it starts to throb. I think of her coming out of the bathroom in her tiny pj's and then wriggling her ass up against my cock. My breathing starts to get faster, I know I'm losing control quickly. I think of how she blushes when I talk dirty and how she reacted when I said I wanted to tie her up. I think she'd like it, I start to pump my cock faster until I cum really hard.

My heart is beating so fast that I can hardly breathe, but unfortunately my cock is still hard, I'm not satisfied yet. I picture her on her knees sucking my cock, fondling my balls and then turning those beautiful eyes upwards to look into mine. This picture forming in my mind sends me over the top once again. God I'm in trouble with Kammie!

6 Kammie

When Luca left I stood leaning my forehead against the door for a long time. What happened last night? I don't think I understand it. Luca is a wonderful guy: he's polite, chivalrous, so bloody handsome and he knows how to treat a lady. God I wanted him so much last night, hell who am I kidding I wanted him all day today as well. Damn Felix and Tasha ruining something that could be great. Well for one night anyway.

I go to bed early because I'm really tired, it was a long night last night. When I get up on Monday, I'm in a bit of a daze, I can't stop thinking about Luca, I need to shake him from my mind. I know I can't talk to Tasha about it because she doesn't want me to get involved with him, I hate hiding things from her, she's my best friend and best friends tell each other everything - right?

I go to work today - I work in a PR and Event Company, Social Butterfly Events, I love my job and I've worked there for years. I love the other members of staff and have made some good friends. One of the girls, Jenny, asks if I want to go to lunch in the pub today because she thinks I look a bit sad, I say yes because I need to talk to someone.

I meet Jenny in reception and we go to TGI's for lunch, it's quick and easy and we can talk. "You look sad today Kammie, is everything alright?" she says as we sit down to order.

"Yeah I'm fine, it's just I met this guy at the weekend." I start to say.

"Ooh tell me more I love your stories on a Monday, they're always juicy" she laughs.

I laugh in return "Well this isn't juicy, Jenny. He is absolutely gorgeous, like I was drooling gorgeous. I think he liked me too because we spent the night together and it was amazing and we didn't even have sex." I look up and I can see Jenny has her mouth wide open. "He's off limits though, not because he's in a relationship but because he's Tasha's boyfriend's best friend and because we both like to play the field they think that if it goes wrong then it will make it awkward for them. I understand what they're saying, but I really felt a connection with him, one like I haven't felt before." I go on to tell her what we talked about and how we spent the night and then the next day.

"You know Kammie, I've never seen you like this about a guy before, it's quite scary. Why don't you just talk to Tasha? She's your best friend she would understand."

"The thing is though Jenny she's right, if we slept together then that would be that and it could get awkward when we all go out again and one of us sleeps with someone else. I know Tasha and Felix are on the road to getting serious and I don't want to spoil that for her. I think I'll just have to make do with flirting with the guy!"

"Well I still think you're mad, I know Tasha and I know she would tell you to go for it and bugger the consequences, if you really like him that won't matter."

"No, I can't tell her Jenny, it will all work out somehow" I say feeling sad.

We go back to work and the rest of the

day drags in, I go home, make a snack to eat and watch a movie, I just can't concentrate though and I start thinking about Luca. I've not dated the same guy more than once for about 4 years, I decided that relationships were too much like hard work and vowed that I would just have one night stands and that satisfied me until now. I don't know why Luca makes me feel like this because from what I understand he is just like me, he sleeps his way through the girls at the gym and always takes a different girl home Friday, Saturday and even Sunday nights.

While I'm zoned out my phone beeps with a text, it's probably Tasha because I haven't texted her today, which is highly unusual, but I didn't want to talk to her. I check my phone and it's a text from Luca, I can feel my heartbeat starting to increase, what does he want? I open the text:

Hey Kammie, how was your day? I slept for most of it, for some reason I didn't sleep much over the weekend ;-)

I hold my phone for a few minutes thinking about what I'm going to reply.

Hey, I had to go to work today, so I'm wrecked now. What kept you awake? I'm sure I heard you snoring lol

Oh fighting talk! I didn't sleep well

because someone was rubbing their cute ass all over me in their sleep ;-)

Ha ha well someone kept me pulled tight into them so that I couldn't move away

Touché baby, touché. How was your day anyway?

Boring, I was so tired I couldn't concentrate, Monday's are always bad days lol

Are you doing anything tonight?

Tonight? Luca its 9.30pm of course I'm not doing anything, it's a school night ;-)

Do you want to go for a coffee? Tonight?

It's late Luca, I shouldn't really

I know I need to spend some time away from him because he's all I think about.

I'm watching a film, I think I'd better stay in

I hear the doorbell ring, who is here at this time of night? I put my phone down on the table and go to open the door. When I do I get a shock, it's Luca standing there with a big grin on his face.

"What are you doing here Luca? It's late!" I'm standing looking at him and realise I haven't invited him in. I stand back and open the door wider, he comes in and I close the door behind him.

"I wanted to see you and I knew you wouldn't want to go out on a school night so I decided to come to you instead." I then notice he has two takeaway cups and a brown paper bag. I look up at him, god he's gorgeous so I smile.

"Is that what I think it is?" I smile "Come on let's get a plate" I can smell the apple pie before I even take it out of the bag.

He follows me into the kitchen and I get the plates out and a fork each, once the pie is on the plates we go back into the lounge, he sits down next to me and I can feel his thigh rubbing against my leg. We talk about what we have done during the day, I tell him about my lunch with Jenny and we laugh a lot.

"So, Kammie, I wanted to see you tonight, I don't know why I just did. I hope you don't mind me coming over this late, I needed to hear you laughing, it does something to my soul" he says putting his plate down on the table. When he sits back on the couch he rests his arm on the couch behind me, I can feel myself blushing and

my heart is racing.

"I don't mind Luca, it's good to see you and you make me laugh. I'm tired though and I know you don't work on a Tuesday but I do, I really need to go to bed." I can see he is really disappointed, after the effort he made to see me tonight, I don't really want to push him away. I take a deep breath and say "If you want to stay with me tonight you can, but no funny business" I laugh. I look up into his eyes and see he is smiling, even his eyes are smiling too.

"I'd love that Kammie, but I will hold you and talk to you, if you fall asleep that's ok too! I just want to spend time with you!" he says standing up and holding his hand out for me to take so that he can pull me up off the couch.

I turn the lights off and lock the front door and he gently pulls me up the stairs, I don't know what is happening between us but I like it. Luca is so not the person that Tasha described, she said he is a lovely person but he's a player, I can see that but there is more to him than that. Luca is someone I could fall in love with if he continues to treat me like this, that scares me. A lot!

7 Luca

As I pull Kammie up the stairs I wonder what the hell I'm doing? Why did I come here? Then I think back to earlier today when I woke up at noon and the bed felt empty, I moved my hands up and down the bed in front of me before I realised I was in my own bed and not hers. I felt empty like a part of me was missing, I don't like that feeling, I've never felt it before. I don't understand it because I didn't even have sex or do anything sexual, I must be losing my mind.

We go into her bedroom and like last time she goes into the bathroom to change for bed, I take my clothes off but I leave my boxers on and slide into her bed. The funny thing is that it doesn't feel weird or awkward, it feels natural. I had intended staying away until the next time we all went out, but I just couldn't do it, I needed to see her.

She comes out of the bathroom all fresh looking with no makeup on, she really is beautiful. "You look beautiful tonight Kammie" I can't believe I said that out loud, but the smile and blush she gives me is well worth it, although my cock starts twitching in my boxers, he just won't behave.

"Why thank you sir" she says blushing. Oh god that makes my cock get even harder. I pull the covers back on her side of the bed and she climbs in next to me. We lay looking at the ceiling for a couple of minutes and then I say "Kammie come here, I want to hold you, please."

She looks at me and smiles and then turns onto her side and wriggles her bum back until the whole of her body is touching mine. It fits perfect, it's like two jigsaw pieces fitting together to make a whole.

"Have you heard from Tasha today?" I ask.

"No I didn't it's strange really because I usually do. She must be wrapped up in Felix." She says sighing.

"Yeah I haven't heard from Felix either"

I say smelling her hair, she smells gorgeous.

"Do you think they would really go mad if they knew you stayed on Saturday night?" she asks.

"I don't know Kammie, I know what they mean by it could be awkward, but to be honest I don't think they should dictate what we do in our lives." I say nuzzling into her ear.

"Mmmm I know, but I don't want Tasha to fall out with me either Luca" I can hear she's getting drowsy and I can feel her body starting to relax, she shuffles her bum back a little bit more until her ass cheeks are on either side of my cock. God she has to stop doing that because I just want to push myself between those cheeks and hear her scream my name.

"Kammie I know that too, but I also know that one night with you wouldn't be enough for me, I know I'd want more, I already want more!" It's silent, great she must have fallen asleep.

"Me too Luca, me too" she whispers, she slowly rolls to face me and kisses me so tenderly on my lips, it takes great control not to push her onto her back and show her how much I want her. I'm not sure I can keep doing this, but then on the other hand I love this, it's special. She pulls away and then rolls back around and wriggles until her ass is resting where it belongs - on either side of my cock. I smile to myself and I can feel myself drifting away.

In the morning I wake up the same as yesterday, to an empty bed and I start feeling for Kammie, she's not there! I feel an immediate sense of loss and jump out of bed to make sure she's ok.

When I fling the bathroom door open to see if she's in there I catch her walking out of the shower reaching for a towel. She lets out a squeal "Oh my god Kammie I'm sorry, I thought you'd gone without saying goodbye and I panicked." I've covered my eyes but I'm still stood there and I can smell her, it's all around the bathroom.

"Luca you don't need to cover your eyes I've got my towel on! You frightened me, I'm not used to someone coming into the bathroom" she chuckles. "Your face is a picture Luca, on the one hand your eyes are out on stalks because you saw me naked and on the other hand you're embarrassed, not something I thought I could associate with you." She is holding her stomach because she is laughing so much.

"Kammie, seriously it doesn't matter whether my eyes are open or closed I can still see you naked" I laugh.

"I hope that's not a bad thing Luca" she says blushing.

"No way baby it's a good thing, I can have that picture in my mind when I go to work today" I smile.

"What are you like Luca?" She turns her back to me and starts putting her make up on. I sit on the lid of the toilet watching her and we talk about what we are both up to today.

She leaves the bathroom and I jump in the shower, I have to have it turned down cold because I really can still see her naked and it's turning me on.

When I get dressed and go downstairs she has made me a cup of coffee. "I have to go Luca, you can stay until you need to go just pull the door behind you when you leave ok" she smiles up at me.

I close the distance between us and put my finger on her chin so that she has to raise it to look at me, she is so beautiful when she looks embarrassed. "I'm sorry" I say and I can see the confusion in her eyes.

I smile and then I kiss her, I just had to taste her again, but this time I take hold of her ass cheeks and lift her up, I take her thighs and I spread them so they are wrapped around my waist. I hear her groan, or is it me? I'm not quite sure. I move to push her up against the wall and continue kissing her, my cock is straining in my jeans; I need to stop this before I lose control.

I pull away, groaning "I'm sorry Kammie I just couldn't help myself."

She smiles "I was waiting for you to do that since you walked in the door last night Luca."

I've still got her wrapped around my waist and I rest my forehead on hers "I'm in so much trouble where you are concerned Kammie. I need to stay away from you because I want you so much I'm afraid I'm just going to take you." I'm panting and I can feel my heart beating really fast.

"I want you to take me Luca, so much" she says closing her eyes.

"I know you have to go Kammie, but this conversation is not over." I kiss her quickly this time, I want to devour her, but I know I can't.

"Ok Luca, let me know when you're ready to talk" she says unwrapping her legs from around my waist, I still have hold of her ass and she slides down my body rubbing my cock as she goes. When she feels it she looks upwards and into my eyes "Mmmm I think you need a cold shower before you go Luca" she says and then when I release her she turns, walks towards the door and when she gets to the door she turns and says "Don't make too much mess" and she walks through the door.

I stand there for a few minutes, and let out the breath I was holding. I then go up the stairs to her bedroom and turn the shower on. I strip my clothes off and get into the shower. I put one hand on the wall, lean against it, I take my other hand and wrap it around my bulging cock. I pump it up and down vigorously until I eventually cum. I don't feel sated like I usually do, this is bad news. I wash myself, then I dry myself off and get dressed. I clean up the bedroom and when I get downstairs I do the same to the kitchen.

I stand there for a few minutes looking around and then I find a pen and paper and write her a note.

Kammie, I have really enjoyed the last few days with you, more than you realise. I think I need to stay away from you for a while because I can feel that you would not be a one night stand for me, I already feel the need to devour you, to help you breathe, and to love you. I don't think either of us are ready for that right now, I know we can be friends and I will text you later to make sure you get home ok love Luca xx

I hope she takes the note the right way, I walk out of her front door and into my car. I drive to work and my mind is working overtime thinking about Kammie and how much I want her. I spend most of the day thinking about her, I help out in the weight room and only have a couple of classes. While I'm in the spinning class I come to the conclusion that I need to go out and get pissed and have a one night stand, that will get her out of my head. Right?

When I'm driving home I think about ringing Glen to see does he want to go out on Friday night, so we can pick up some women. I smile to myself thinking that I have the perfect solution. When I get home I drop my gym bag on the floor and then I pick up my phone and text Kammie.

Hey, hope you understand what I meant about the note and you don't hate me, friends?

She doesn't answer back straight away and I pace up and down my kitchen waiting for her to reply.

Hey Luca, yeah I understand, it's fine, it's better this way. I'll see you around x

No way am I leaving it like that! Is she for real?

Kammie, I can't say this politely but I want to fuck your brains out and then I want to take you in my arms and never let you go. That scares me so much, I have NEVER felt like this about anyone and I'm not sure I'm ready for this, yet! You are more than a one night stand to me, I know that I would fall in love with you so easily and I'm scared. Don't just shrug me off with a "see you around", please Kammie.

I don't get a response, now I'm worried I've upset her, crap what am I going to do now? I said I wouldn't go round, I said I would stay away from her for a while, crap - how did I get into this mess?

8 Kammie

When I got home from work and saw Luca's note, I was annoyed, it made me feel cheap and we hadn't even had sex together. Maybe we should have just had sex and then it would be out of our systems and we could get on with our lives.

When he text me, I admit I was still upset, I didn't want to let him get away with it that lightly. So when he sent me his next text, I collapsed onto the floor sobbing, why tell me these things and then take it all away from me without me actually having had it. What can I say in response?

I sit on the floor sobbing when Tasha

rings, I sniff and then try and compose myself "Hey Tasha, how's things?"

"I'm good Kammie, what's wrong are you ok? You sound like you've been crying. Will I come over to you?"

"God no Tasha I'm fine, I just dropped something on my foot and it hurt, you caught me as it just landed on my toe." That's twice I've lied to her in as many days. We never lie to each other, we never hide anything from each other. Now I feel guilty!

"As long as you're sure. Just a minute Kammie, yes Felix I'm on the phone, I'm talking to Kammie. What do you mean why? She's my friend silly. Sorry about that Kammie, I was wondering if you want to go out Friday night just the two of us, we haven't done that in a while. Felix you can go out with Luca or someone else, look just wait until I've finished talking to Kammie. God Kammie he's a moaner he keeps talking. Look I'll have to go but we will do something Friday ok."

"Ok Tasha, tell Felix to butt out ha ha, yeah talk to you in the week bitch" I say getting up off the floor. I hang up the phone and stare at it, what am I going to say to Luca now?

I start to dial his number because I think

it's better if I talk to him instead of texting him, just as it starts to ring I hear a knock at my door. I smile to myself because Luca must have come round to talk instead of waiting for me to ring, he really is impatient.

When I open the door I have a big smile on my face and then it drops, it's not Luca, it's the guy from Saturday night. How does he know where I live? He must have followed us or something. "Hello, how can I help you?" I say pretending I don't recognise him.

He doesn't say a word, he just pushes the door open and pushes past me. "Well hello there, don't you remember me? You were promising me a good night on Saturday and then you left with someone else, so I decided I still want a good time." Before I know it he has closed the door, pushed me up against it and he is trying to kiss me. Holy crap! What do I do now? I do what most girls would do in this situation, I cry!

He's still trying to put this tongue down my throat and I've got tears coming down my face. "Leave me alone, get out" I'm shouting into his mouth as I'm twisting my head to get away from him. I suddenly realise what could happen here and I lift my leg up and knee him in the balls. When he bends over to hold himself, I open the door and run. All I can hear is him shouting at me, I don't know what he's saying because I just want to get away from him. I can hear my name being shouted, I know I didn't give him my name. It's then I realise it's from my phone, I obviously didn't hang up when I rang Luca.

"Luca, Luca" I cry "Help me please" I'm still running.

"Kammie I'm just around the corner, I'll be there in a minute, stay calm" he's talking to me the whole time and then I see his car coming round the corner and he screeches to a stop and flies out of the car and wraps himself around me. "What the hell happened Kammie, where is he? Get in the car and I'll take you home" he says as he walks me to his car, he puts his arm around my shoulder pulling me in tight.

He puts me in the front seat and puts my seat belt on for me, he then goes around the other side of the car and climbs in. He holds my hand all the way home and then he locks me in the car while he goes into the house to see if the man has gone. He comes out a few minutes later and says he's gone, he opens the door and helps me out. I'm shaking like a leaf.

"Why me Luca? What did he want from me?" I'm crying.

"Shh Kammie, come on you're not

staying here tonight, let's pack you a bag for tonight and tomorrow." He takes me into the house and helps me pack a bag, I feel helpless. I've always been independent and it's hard knowing that I don't want to be alone and I'm afraid to be in my house.

When we are getting back into Luca's car he holds my hand as he drives me to his apartment. I follow him inside and I'm surprised, I thought that because he wasn't expecting someone it would be messy, but it's not, it's immaculate. I'm gob smacked! "Wow Luca, your place is fabulous, not what I expected at all" I smile at him.

He laughs "did you expect clothes all over the place and empty beer cans everywhere." He winks at me, god that's so sexy.

"Yeah I did actually" I say turning on the spot looking around.

He chuckles and then takes my bag into one of the rooms off the kitchen. "Come on let's have something to eat" he says and I sit up on a bar stool while he prepares a chicken Caesar salad. He is gorgeous and even more so when he concentrates on cooking, I can see his muscles in his arms flexing as he's cooking the chicken.

How did I end up here with Luca? We are

supposed to be spending time apart, what will I do now?

Luca

I can't believe I brought Kammie back to my apartment, I'm supposed to be staying away from her, she is so intoxicating I feel like I'm drowning in her when I'm near her. I can't think straight, this is a bad idea, but what was I to do?

When I saw her number ringing me I thought about not picking up, but then I couldn't do that to her and I needed to hear her voice again. As I went to speak I could hear her shouting at someone and screaming, I panicked, kept the phone turned on and jumped in the car and drove to her house, I kept calling her name hoping she would hear me. When she finally answered me she was uncontrollable and I told her I was nearby. As I got closer to her house, I could see her, I flew out of the car to get her and I took her in my arms while she sobbed. My heart was breaking for her, she is such a confident independent woman and for something like this to happen is just unbelievable.

I got her in the car and we drove to her house, I went inside because I wanted to check he wasn't still there, I don't know what I would have done to him if he had been, I don't want to think about it.

After we get her clothes together I bring her back to my apartment and it's only when I'm cooking dinner that I stop to think about what I've done. I can't get her out of my head and bringing her here was not my best plan, but I need to make sure she is ok tonight, we can talk about what happens next later.

"Do you mind eating at the breakfast bar? It's where I normally eat" I smile at her, it feels strange cooking for her in my apartment, I never entertain anyone here.

"That's fine Luca, your apartment is lovely, you must have been here for a while."

"Yes I've been here about 5 years and I love it." I say passing her her plate. We sit and eat our dinner and pass small talk about our jobs and where we've lived, after dinner she helps me to wash the dishes and put everything away. It feels very domesticated, it feels scary because it feels natural. I shake my head to try and get these thoughts out of them.

"Let's go and sit in the lounge and see what's on the TV" I automatically reach out for her hand and pull her to follow me, I can see her smiling.

When we sit on the couch, my leg is touching hers and I can feel the heat rising up my body, when she moves slightly I can feel my cock twitching. I smile because she feels so good.

"Can I ask you something Kammie? If you're offended you don't have to answer but I'm just curious" I'm nervous because this could go one of two ways and one of them would be bad.

"Of course you can Luca" she says resting her head on my shoulder "I've seen you almost naked for god's sake, so you shouldn't be embarrassed asking a question" she giggles, god I wish she'd stop that, it does things to my insides.

"I know we need to talk about what happened earlier and we will later when we go to bed and you're relaxed" I smile "I know we need to talk about my note and what happened after, but there's plenty of time for that" she smiles at me, but I can see the confusion in her eyes, she obviously thought that's what I wanted to talk about.

"I know that you like one night stands, the same as I do because I'm not ready for commitment yet. However, I have a couple of things that I like sexually and I wanted to know how you feel about them." I stop talking and look her in the eye, I've turned my body to face her. She sits back a bit obviously confused by the question.

"O K" she says slowly "this sounds serious and something that I'm not going to like" her smile leaves her face.

"Don't worry it's nothing bad, it's just .... You know I enjoy sex, but I sometimes enjoy a different type of sex." I can see I've got her attention, she looks confused.

"I like to control sexually" when I say it out loud it sounds dirty "nothing really heavy, but I like to dominate in the bedroom, I very rarely lose control. I like a woman who wants to do what I want her to do, if that makes sense". I look at her and her eyes are wide open, I decide to keep going before I chicken out. "I'm not a Dom or anything looking for a submissive, I just like to make a woman happy and control her pleasure. That gives me the best orgasms ever." I stop talking and look at her, she is red in the face. "Kammie talk to me, say something." I don't know what I'll do if she hates me now.

9 Kammie

I feel like I'm stood in front of a lion and I don't know whether to run or stand still. Luca has just told me he likes to dominate in the bedroom, I don't know why he told me that seeing as we aren't going to have a relationship, but I just don't know what say.

"Kammie talk to me, say something" Luca is pleading with me to say something.

I take a deep breath and say "ok can I ask you some questions Luca?" he's sitting facing me on the couch, with one leg bent under him and his arm resting on the back of the couch.

"You can ask anything you want Kammie" he says smiling a little, I think he thought I would run out the door.

"Are you into wearing leather and shit like that?" I'm trying not to laugh because it's a ridiculous question.

He laughs back at me "No Kammie, I don't like wearing leather" he smiles and god he's gorgeous.

"Do you use whips and things?" I can feel myself gulping for breath, these are things that repulse me, but I can feel myself getting turned on.

No I don't use whips or things, I would be partial to tying you up though" he winks at me.

I laugh "Ok well that doesn't sound bad so why are you telling me anyway?"

He looks me deep in the eyes, smiles and then says "Just for future reference."

I laugh loudly and throw my head back, he joins in with me and the tension from earlier is lifted. I don't tell him that I'm always domineering in the bedroom too, but only because I don't want someone to steal my heart, it makes it easier to walk away. I've always wanted a man to come into my life who dominates me and makes me do what he wants in the bedroom instead of me having to think of positions etc. I don't tell him any of this!

We watch TV for a bit longer and then we go to bed, it's become a habit already that I slide into the bed and he pulls me close to him. I've never had this closeness with a man before, I really like it. Maybe I should consider a relationship, maybe that's what I need instead of one night stands all the time.

We talk about the man who came to the house, and what I'm going to do about it.

When we wake up in the morning we go down and have a cup of coffee, we talk about Luca's note and we both agree that we should stay away from each other for a while and then maybe our attraction will have worn off. I find it hard being in the same room as him and not jump on him to be honest.

It's the right thing to do for Tasha and Felix, I can see that Tasha loves Felix a lot and I know their relationship will last, they are getting very serious and we agreed that it's for the best, because it could be awkward.

We don't see each other for a few months after I leave his house that morning. We text sometimes but we haven't met up, I miss him not being with me, especially in my bed where he always cuddled me, but I know it's for the best!

10 Luca

6 Months Later

Today is Felix's wedding to Tasha, he's a lucky man, she's gorgeous and such a beautiful person. It also means that I'm going to see Kammie again. I haven't seen her for about 6 months and it's been hard to stay away, maybe now Felix and Tasha are getting married, we can hook up.

When I see her walking down the aisle in front of Tasha, she is all I can see, she is beautiful, she takes my breath away. I realise how much I missed her, my body is responding and I can feel my cock growing and pushing against my zip. I try to adjust myself discreetly.

She smiles at me and all I want to do is to push her up against the altar, fuck her and devour her lips. She really is affecting me badly. I mouth "you look beautiful" to her, she blushes and then she giggles, oh my god that really turns me on. My trousers are really uncomfortable now, what am I going to do?

I can't stop looking at her, I keep my eyes on her during the whole of the service, every time she catches me looking at her she blushes, this is my dream right here.

When we walk back down the aisle together, she links my arm, I put my free hand over hers which is hooked over my arm "It's really good to see you Kammie, you look beautiful, you took my breath away."

"Thanks Luca, you don't look bad yourself" she giggles, I obviously make her nervous. I like that because it must mean she likes me and that means we have a chance.

Kammie

I didn't realise how much my body would react to seeing Luca, I've had sex with other guys since we met, but I always see his face when I'm with them. I can't seem to shake his image out of my mind. When I saw him stood at the altar it felt like I was walking up to marry him, I couldn't see anyone else but Luca.

When we walked back down the aisle and he told me I was beautiful I nearly came on the spot. He looks so handsome and I know I won't be able to keep away from him today. I know I'll end up in his bed because there is no way I'm letting anyone else get into it. That is a sure thing!!

I don't care what Tasha and Felix say, they will be occupied tonight and won't notice what goes on around them, I've decided that I want Luca and I intend on getting him whether it is tonight or in the near future. He will be mine!

After all the speeches are finished and out of the way, Tasha and Felix walk around talking to everyone and so do we. When they are called up to do their first dance to Shania

Twain – From This Moment, me and Luca have to dance with them.

I'm watching Tasha and Felix start their dance, I'm smiling because they look so happy and I can see how much they love each other. All of a sudden, Luca comes up behind me and whispers in my ear "Are you ready beautiful? I want to hold you tight when we dance, I want you to feel what you do to me Kammie."

I shudder when he's finished talking, he is really turning me on and I can feel myself getting wet between my legs. I say quietly "I'm always ready for you Luca, you can hold me tight anytime" and then I turn around and reach to grab his hand to pull him on the dance floor when the DJ says it is time for the best man and the matron of honour to dance.

I risk looking at his face and I am rewarded by the most amazing grin that reaches from one eye to the other. It's when I'm this close that I notice he has dimples when he smiles, god I want to lick them.

Luca looks like the original bad boy, he has dark hair, blue eyes and he has loads of tattoos, some of which are noticeable. He is far from a bad boy, he has never been in trouble with the police and you realise that you can't judge a book by its cover with him.

We stand on the dance floor looking at each other, he puts one hand on the base of my spine, pulls me in close, then he takes my hand and holds it up in line with my shoulder. I can feel the warmth coming off his body and I shiver "Are you cold Kammie?" he asks smiling and pulling me even closer.

I laugh because I don't know what to say, "No you're doing a good job of warming me up Luca" he laughs and starts moving me around the dance floor. Who knew that Luca could dance like a ballroom dancer?

When the dance finishes I look up to him and smile "I'm thirsty Luca, I need to go and get a drink. Do you want one?"

He looks deep into my eyes and says "I don't think you can move yet Kammie, I think I need to keep you just where you are."

I'm confused until he pulls me that bit closer and I can feel why he doesn't want me to move, he would have to explain the bulge in his trousers. I giggle and he growls into my ear, "Stop giggling Kammie that will only make it worse. STOP!"

His tone vibrates through my body to my toes, it's tingling all my nerve endings and I can feel myself start to blush, a deep dark red.

"God Kammie, you're making it worse, just talk to me about something unsexy please" he laughs.

"Ok do you see those two old ladies over there on that table? They do ballroom dancing, maybe you should ask them to dance, it might help you with your" I clear my throat "problem" I move away from him and walk off the dance floor towards the bar. When I get to the edge of the dance floor I turn and look over my shoulder at Luca and he is stood there with his mouth wide open. I wink, look down at his crotch and then walk over and order my drink.

When I have my drink in my hand I turn and look on the dance floor and it is my time to stand with my mouth open, Luca is dancing with one of the two old ladies I had pointed out to him. I laugh until I feel tears running down my face, that man never ceases to surprise me.

Luca

I hear laughter and I turn to see Kammie stood on the edge of the dance floor watching me. She looks so gorgeous when she laughs. I smile at her and concentrate on Phyllis, she was telling me she hadn't danced for 2 years since her husband died and was happy when I had asked her to dance. That is so sad and I want her to enjoy her dance, Kammie can wait.

When the song is over I turn around to go and find Kammie, she has moved, I can't see her. I need to find her, I don't want to lose her to someone else tonight, or any night for that matter.

I see her talking to Glen, he's the last person I want her to talk to, but I don't have any rights over her. I walk towards them and I can hear Glen asking her whether she has a boyfriend at the moment. I stand still where I am, I want to hear her answer, this could be interesting. I know she doesn't date, she's like me she likes uncomplicated, unattached sex.

"Well Glen, it's complicated. I don't date but I do have someone I'm interested in" that's interesting "if it doesn't work out later on and I'm looking for some fun, I know where I'll find you" she smiles at him and walks back to the bar. I can't believe how listening to that conversation makes me feel, I never feel jealousy or resentment, but that is exactly how I feel right now.

I walk past Glen and say hi, then I walk

over to the bar and lean next to Kammie "Hey there, having fun?" she turns to look at me and she smiles her beautiful smile.

"Do you want a drink Luca? You look like you were having fun on the dance floor, I bet you're thirsty" she winks at me, god what I want to do to her right now.

"I'd love a drink thanks Kammie, can I have a JD and Coke, I think it's time to get on the hard stuff."

She giggles "Ok tough guy" she orders my drink and one for herself. "Come on then Luca, let's have a toast" she says clinking her glass with mine, "To friends not having sex."

I look at her and say "To friends not having sex" and then I wink at her. She blushes and I lean down towards her ear and I growl "Do you want to stay with me later and not have sex?"

I see her eyes sparkle when she whispers "I'd love to Luca" we clink glasses again, never taking our eyes off each other.

We say silent for a while and then we both start laughing, that sets the tone for the evening and we have lots of fun together, dancing, drinking and chatting.

11 Kammie

I've had so much fun tonight, Luca is amazing, he is so funny and so gorgeous to look at too.

I hear the music stop and Felix and Tasha are on the stage, Felix says "Ladies and gentlemen, thank you for coming along to celebrate our marriage, Natasha and I wish you all the best but we are leaving early in the morning so we will be leaving now". They look so happy, I feel a bit jealous, it's a strange feeling for me and I shake my head to get rid of that thought. Tasha smiles at me when she walks past me and I smile back, she is glowing.

I feel someone slip their hand into mine and I turn and look at Luca "They look happy don't they" he says, I nod, I feel emotional. He pulls me onto the dance floor "Come on let's dance". Thankfully it's a fast song and we fall about laughing and dancing at the same time. We notice that everyone is leaving, we must have been dancing for an hour, wow that went really fast.

"Come on baby let's go to bed and not have sex" Luca says and I fall about the place laughing. "What are you laughing at?" he says pulling me along behind him as we go up the stairs.

"Does that chat up line work for you Luca?" I say laughing so hard I can hardly get my words out.

He stops suddenly and I bump into him, he turns slowly. I gulp! "I'll tell you in the morning" he says as he leans down and takes my bottom lip and sucks it, all the time keeping eye contact. I groan. He pushes me up against the wall in the hallway and puts his two hands on either side of my head, he looks down at me and then down to my lips, then back up to my eyes. He moves so very slowly, I want him to hurry up, I'm silently trying to hurry him up. His lips eventually touch mine, ever so gently, he just grazes them, but they feel like they are on fire.

I groan and reach out to grab him and pull him closer to me. He pulls back and takes my hand again "Come on baby, I want you in my bed, undressed and pulled close against me, we can continue this in my room". I can feel my heart racing. I let him pull me down the corridor, until we come to his room, he takes out his room card and opens the door.

He doesn't turn the lights on, he pulls me through the door and closes it behind me. He pushes me up against the door "I've wanted to kiss you all night Kammie, I don't think you know what you do to me" I don't get chance to reply as he leans down and devours my lips. God he's a good kisser!

I start to undo his buttons on his shirt while he is kissing me, I feel frantic, I feel like I need him to be naked. "No Kammie, leave my clothes, I'll take them off when I'm ready. I want to take yours off for you."

He kisses me and then places small kisses on my face towards my ear, then he takes my lobe in his mouth, god I love it when he does that. He then kisses along my collar bone and turns me to face the door at the same time. I feel exposed, vulnerable and so turned on. He continues to kiss me as he undoes the zip on my dress, when the zip is open he slides the dress off me.

All of a sudden the light turns on full blast, I groan and close my eyes. In between kisses Luca says "Open your eyes Kammie, I want you to watch me." I look over my shoulder as he kisses down my back over my corset, down over my panties, my stockings and suspenders and then he turns me around. He slowly takes each leg and lifts it out of my dress and moves my dress to one side. He kisses up my leg, the front of my panties, up over my suspender belt and up towards my stomach. All the time he is looking me in the eye, I am too turned on to look away.

"Luca" I whisper, "Luca" I groan.

He continues moving up my stomach "Mmm you smell good Kammie, I really want to taste you." When he reaches my breasts he swiftly moves his hand around to my back and expertly undoes all the hooks on my corset and when he has undone the last one, it falls to the floor. He stops what he is doing and takes one step back "Wow baby you are so beautiful" he moves forward so quick I didn't even notice and he takes one of my nipples in his mouth.

"God Luca what are you doing to me?" I groan, I don't know if I can take anymore, I am so wet.

"I'm tasting you baby, I want to see if you taste as good as you smell" he moves up to my mouth and kisses me so hard I nearly cum on the spot. "I'm going to lift you up, wrap your legs around me" he growls into my mouth. I don't have time to think about what he is doing because his hands are lifting me by my ass. I do as he asked and wrap my legs around him.

Luca

I want her so much, more than I've ever wanted anything in my life. She did what I asked and she is now wrapped around me wearing nothing but her panties, stockings and suspenders. I have to take a breath and think about what is going to happen tonight.

This is a test for both of us, can I go through the night without fucking her? It will be hard but I need to show her that I have restraint. That doesn't mean that I can't taste her, love her, consume her.

"Hold tight baby I'm going to move to the bed" I say pulling her in tighter. She tightens her grip on my waist with her legs. God that is such a turn on, she has a great grip, imagine ..... No stop it Luca, stop.

I get to the bed and I lay her down gently. I stand back up but lean over her and slowly take her panties down, I can smell her on them, it only makes me want her more. I do the same to remove her stockings and suspenders, she is now naked on my bed, just liked I've dreamed since the night I met her.

I stand up and look at her, she doesn't shy away like some girls would, she just looks me in the eye and smiles "This is all a bit one sided Luca" so she sits up and starts to take my clothes off.

"No lay back down" I say and she does it straight away, she is going to kill me tonight by doing what I tell her with no questions asked.

I slowly undo my buttons on my shirt and take it off. I hear her gasp when she sees my tattoos. I know she's seen them before but it was dark and she wasn't this turned on. I undo my top buttons on my trousers, then the zip and then I let them fall to the floor.

"Oh my god Luca you were naked under there all night?" She blushes and I see her lick her lips but I don't think she realised she did it.

I smile at her "Yes I was baby, you like what you see?"

"Yes I do, very much so" she says still licking her lips. God I feel like I am going to explode and she hasn't even touched me yet!

I step out of my trousers and deliberately move very slowly towards her, I work my way up her body again, this time kissing and licking her inch by inch until I come to her sweet spot between her legs. I look up at her face and she is leaning up on her elbows so she can watch me, most girls would hide so they couldn't watch. I knew she was going to be different.

Her eyes open wide and she looks from my eyes and down to my hands which are slowly moving towards her lips. She gasps and holds her breath when I open them and feel that she is really wet, her smell is so overpowering. I have to taste her, I move my face closer to her and then I stick my tongue out and in between her lips. I groan, she tastes delicious! I hear her groan at the same time.

I plunge a finger inside her at the same time as sucking on her clit, she lifts her ass so that her pussy is closer to my face, I chuckle.

"Seriously Luca, don't' laugh, it'll send me into orbit" she says throwing herself back down on the bed.

I try to hold back on the laughing, I don't want this to end just yet. I take my finger out and then plunge two of them in, she moans. I continue to lick her clit and then I take my fingers out and plunge my tongue inside her.

"Luca, oh my god Luca, please" she pleads with me.

"Please what Kammie?" I say when I take my tongue back out "What?" I say commandingly "Say it, say it!"

"Luca please let me cum" she groans, I laugh, I plunge two fingers back inside and then I flick my tongue over her clit. She starts arching her back so she can get closer and then I can feel her walls clamping over my fingers and she shouts out my name. God that feels good to hear my name coming from her lips.

I give her a minute to calm down and then I crawl up her body and devour her mouth, I want her to share her taste. I can feel her hands running down my back towards my ass, if she starts touching me then I won't be able to show restraint. I take one hand and reach behind me and stop her hands, she groans. I then lift her hands above her head and start kissing down her neck towards her breasts.

"Luca, I want to touch you please, I want to give you what you gave me" she whispers.

"No Kammie, I can't let you touch me, I won't be able to control myself, I want you so bad, but we agreed no sex" I hate saying it.

"No way Luca you can't say that after what you just did to me. Please Luca I need to feel you inside me" she isn't making this easy for me and I can hear she is getting upset.

"Baby" I say rolling off her and pulling her close to me "we said no sex tonight, so that's what we are going to do. It will happen, just not tonight ok?"

She starts struggling to get away from me "Luca let me go, I want to go to my own room."

"No way Kammie, no way. You are staying with me tonight, I need to have you close to me. Please don't pull away from me baby, please" she stops struggling. I hear her sigh really heavily. She's given in, she's laid on her side with the whole of the back side of her body against mine, I can see the goosebumps on her skin, I reach across and pull the covers over us. "Kammie, I can't explain to you how I feel about you because

I have never had these feelings before. When I have a woman in my bed, I can't wait to get them out of it and out of my life. With you I want more, I want you in my bed, but I need you to know that it isn't only for sex. I want more baby." I lean down and kiss her on the nape of her neck.

I think she is crying because I can feel her body shaking. "Kammie what's wrong, come on stop crying." I wrap my arms around her, I wrap my leg over hers, I can't get any closer to her without being inside her.

"Luca what you did to me was so amazing, I just don't understand why you don't want me." Did I just hear her right? I told her I want her, why does she think I don't?

I move backwards until she lays flat on her back, then I straddle her and pin her hands above her head. "Kammie I want you so bad, we made a promise to Tasha and Felix and I know that we probably don't need to worry about that because they just got married, but I need you to know that you are not like the rest of the women that I take home at the end of the night. The only way for me to show you that you are different, that you mean something to me, is by not having sex with you tonight. I know that is all kinds of fucked up but that is me Kammie, fucked up."

I lean down and kiss her, I need her to feel my emotions right now. Luckily she kisses me back and I release her hands, she quickly puts them around my back and pulls me closer. I can feel my cock starting to get hard again and it's pushing against her, I need to move.

I pull away gently and then roll back onto my side and pull her close to me. "Kammie, I've really enjoyed tonight and I sure want to do it again" I nuzzle into her neck.

"Me too Luca, me too" I can hear she is starting to drift off, I love sleeping with my body wrapped around her, it feels a little bit like heaven.

12 Kammie

Tonight has been surreal, I had fun all night with Luca, we laughed, we danced, we started to mess around and then he rejected me. That hurt because I know that whenever he takes a woman back to his bed, he never rejects anyone, but he rejected me. That hurts! I know he said that he wants me, but he showed me tonight that he doesn't really want me!

I wait for about an hour until I hear him snoring gently and I can feel his hold on me has loosened, I slowly move his arm and leg off me and then I roll out of the bed. I put my dress on and pick up my shoes and underwear, ready to do the walk of shame. I tiptoe to the door and open it very gently making sure I don't wake Luca.

When I get outside I quietly close the door and then I run down the corridor to my own room. I quickly pack everything into my suitcase that I had brought with me, I leave the room and go down to reception. I pay for my room and then I get a cab home. I have tears down my cheeks, I really wanted Luca to like me, I wanted him to fuck me, I needed to get him out of my system.

When I get home, I jump into the shower and then climb into bed, I make sure my phone is turned off, I don't want anyone to ring me.

When I wake up in the morning, I realise that I need a few days to myself to process what happened yesterday. I know me and Luca had promised Felix and Tasha that we wouldn't hook up, but they are married now so we aren't going to ruin our friendships, although after last night I think it is already ruined. I don't want to see or speak to Luca until I can process what happened. I pack my bag and decide to take a trip, I have family down in Devon, they will let me stay with them for a few days. I had booked some time off work anyway because of the wedding so I can stay with them for a few days. I leave my mobile phone in my bedside table, I don't want any temptation to speak to Luca, I need to work out what is inside my head.

The drive down there takes me about 2 hours and I concentrate on the road rather than what is in my head. I love coming to Torquay, it is known as the English Riviera and it is like being in Spain! I find my Aunty's house and they are happy to see me and tell me that of course I can stay. We have lunch and then I tell them that I want a walk on the beach to clear my head.

Their house is only about 10 minutes from the beach and it's really warm, I walk and stop on the way for an ice cream, then when I get to the beach I sit on the steps looking out to sea. I used to do this as a child and loved just staring at the sea, watching the waves.

I think about Luca and how I ran away instead of facing my fears – my fear of any type of relationship. I must have sat on the steps for quite a while because it starts to get cold, I look around me and don't see anyone for miles.

I get up and walk back to Aunty Susan's house, when I get back she is in the kitchen cooking dinner. "Are you hungry Kammie? I'm just making dinner for Uncle John."

"Yeah the fresh air has made me

quite hungry Aunty Susan" I say standing against the kitchen door. I help her to lay the table and we all sit down.

When we are finished eating Aunty Susan asks me "Why are you here Kammie? Not that we don't like having you, but you don't come down very often and it was such short notice." She smiles at me and lifts one of her eyebrows.

I giggle slightly, she always was astute. "Something happened over the weekend, my friend got married, it was a great wedding but there's this guy and I got spooked and ran. I've never done that in my life, I always face my problems head on so it's been a bit of a shock that I left like that."

"I see" she says "Will we pour a glass of wine and talk about it?" she says as she clears the table.

"Yeah if you don't mind" I help to clear the table and then we take our glasses of wine out into the conservatory. It's still bright out and the conservatory has stored the heat of the day and it is lovely and warm in here.

I take a swig, then a deep breath and start to tell her about Luca. I tell her about how we met, the agreements we made with Tasha and Felix, how we both want more but are afraid to take what we want because neither of us have had relationships. By the time I finish telling her all of this we have polished off a full bottle of wine.

"Kammie, it's your life and no one can tell you how to live it."

I go to bed after we've finished the bottle and when I get into bed I start to feel bad for running away, now I know Luca won't want anything to do with me. I feel myself starting to cry because I want him in my life and I feel sad thinking that he might not want me.

I have a restless sleep, Luca dominates my mind, my subconscious, even my waking thoughts. I get up and have breakfast and decide to go down to the beach again, it's beautiful weather.

I walk to the town centre and have a browse around the shops, the town centre has changed a lot since I was last here on holiday. As I ramble down towards the beach I am lost in thought and I don't hear the car as I am crossing the road. It hits me and I'm thrown backwards onto the curb. The pain in my side is horrible, I sit on the pavement and cry, I cry big fat dirty tears and it's not just for the car that hit me, but for Luca.

The driver gets out of the car and runs

over to me "Oh my god are you ok? You just stepped out in front of me, I slowed down as much as I could" I can hear the panic in his voice.

"I'm fine just a little bruised that's all, it was my fault. I hope there's no damage to your car, I'm sorry" I cry again. He helps me up and then offers to give me a lift somewhere. I shake my head "It's fine I'll be ok, I just need to walk it out, it's more my ego that's bruised" I smile and he gets back in his car and drives off.

It hurts when I walk, but only on my side, I walk slowly and stop at the Belgrave Hotel, opposite the beach and ordered a drink. While I'm waiting, I think about Tasha's day and how good it was and how much fun we had. I drink my drink and then walk over to the beach and I go to the steps and sit on my towel. I put my legs out in front of me and prop myself up on my elbows. This is lovely, it's so peaceful and warm.

After a while it feels cold, then I realise that something is shadowing the sun, I open my eyes under my sunglasses and it takes a while to focus.

"Hello Kammie, what are you doing here?" it's Luca, what the hell!

"Luca?!? How ..... When .... Why ....." I'm speechless, I really don't know what to say.

He sits down next to me and I look at him, he really is gorgeous, I smile a little, because he came here to find me.

"What happened Kammie? Why did you run away from me? I've been so worried about you, when I woke up and you weren't there, I thought you'd gone to freshen up. Then you didn't turn up for breakfast, I waited for 2 hours in reception waiting for you to show up and then I asked the receptionist and she told me you'd checked out during the night.

I was angry because you didn't tell me, I thought we could talk to each other Kammie. I went to your house, you weren't there, your car wasn't there. I asked around, but other than Tasha I don't really know many of your friends. I was just going to leave it like that, you obviously don't care enough about me to tell me what I did wrong." I try to interrupt and he stops me "No Kammie! You need to listen to me, you need to understand how I got here. I sat at your house and you didn't come home, I was so worried I rang the hospitals to find out had you had an accident. I thought you'd been hurt, or worse."

I can feel the tears falling down my face, he did that, all of that for me, because he was worried about me. I'm such a bitch, he must have been petrified.

"This morning when you still weren't home I went to Jean's house to ask her if she knew where you were. She didn't but she rang your mum and asked her. She gave me the details and after I spoke to Aunty Susan, I've been walking up and down this beach all day waiting for you to turn up."

I sit looking at him with my mouth open wide, he did all of that to find me, me - Kammie. I don't know what to say, so I lean closer and kiss him, I can feel all my emotion coming out in this kiss. Luckily he kisses me back, it's full of passion and emotion. I pull back and look at him, he reaches across and pushes the hair off my face, "Kammie, I don't want my world not to have you in it. Life means so much more when you're there. I thought I had explained that and then you ran, that hurt me, that's why I don't do relationships, but I wanted to try with you!"

Oh no I detect the past tense. "Luca are you telling me that you came all the way down here, found me and now you're telling me you don't want to try? I'm confused." I don't understand what he is saying. "I ran because I want a relationship with you and that scares me, I never want relationships, but with you I can feel a deeper connection. When you rejected me sexually that hurt me, you sleep with a lot of women but you didn't want to have sex with me." I feel a lone tear slowing winding its way down my cheek, it reaches my chin when I feel his thumb wipe it up and then I feel his lips kiss me in the spot where the tear was. I sigh.

"Kammie, you need to look at me, take those glasses off, please!" I do as he asks.

"I want to have sex with you right now, every time I'm with you I want to have sex with you, but I feel we are more than that! I want more than sex with you, I want to build our feelings and I want you in my life for longer than one night Kammie. Don't you ever think that I don't want you because I do, more than you'll ever know." He reaches across and puts his hand behind my head in the nape of my neck and pulls me close to him, he rests his head on my forehead. "Kammie I don't know what you did to me, but you make me want everything I have been running away from for so long" he leans forward slowly and takes my lips and devours them, he lays me down and hovers over the top of me. "Baby I want you, but I want all of you, I don't just want sex with you. Do you want that too?"

My heart is beating so fast, I can feel myself hold my breath. "Luca, I want all of that with you, you do things to me that no one else has ever done and I'm talking about my mind not my body" I kiss him, just a quick peck! "I don't know where we go from here Luca but I want to do this together."

"Kammie that's all I want for both of us, we have to try and make this happen. I know that I want this to work, I know that a relationship is new to me but I can't think of anyone else I'd like to have a relationship with. You complete me Kammie." He moves off me and lays next to me. He takes my hand and we don't say anything, we don't need to.

We lay looking at the sky just talking and getting to know each other better.

"Come on Luca it's getting late I need to go back to Aunty Susan's, she'll be wondering where I am." I say sitting up.

Luca stands and holds him hand out to pull me up. "When I spoke to her she told me to take my time, do you think she will let me stay? Or should I book into a hotel for the night, I'm not driving home today. I want to be near you Kammie, I don't want to be away from you, I need to know that you are ok."

I smile and take his hand, when he pulls me to a standing position, I scream out in pain. He drops my hand immediately and looks at me with great concern. "Kammie what's the matter? Did I hurt you I'm sorry."

"I'm fine, I just had an accident earlier, it's only a bruise, look" I say pulling my top up to show him.

"Oh my god Kammie what happened to you baby?" he says touching me gently on my bruise, which is now huge.

"I wasn't looking where I was going, I was thinking about us and I walked in front of a car, he tried to stop but he just tapped me, I fell on the ground, but I'm alright. I just forgot about it until I went to stand up."

"What if something had happened to you Kammie? I don't know what I would have done, we've only just started out life together. Come on I'll help you to walk home." He takes my bags and puts his arm around me, I don't tell him that he doesn't need to do it because I'm glad he does.

When we get back to Aunty Susan's she welcomes us both, she has dinner almost ready, she knew Luca would come back with me, especially after our chat last night.

"Luca you can stay the night if you want, I don't mind so you don't need to stay in a hotel, it's fine" Aunty Susan says.

"Thank you so much Susan I'd like that very much. Kammie has injured herself, she was hit by a car and I want to make sure she is ok" he says taking my hand and placing it in his. I turn towards him and smile.

"Oh my god Kammie are you ok, let me take a look" she says coming over to me. We spend the next half an hour checking me over and deciding whether I need to go to hospital or not. I don't think I need to I just need to take some painkillers that's all. Eventually I convince them and we lay the table for dinner.

Dinner, like last night, was gorgeous and we had a few glasses of wine, Luca gets on very well with Aunty Susan and when I'm helping her to clear the dishes she says "Kammie, I can see why you like him he's a lovely guy, he's gorgeous as well" she laughs "but most of all he cares about you a lot, he never takes his eyes off you and is ready to help you if you were in too much pain."

I feel myself blush "Do you think so? I've never felt like this over a guy before, I usually just see them once and never more than that."

"Well I'd say he's a keeper Hun" she hugs me. "Will you be ok? Do you need any more pain killers?"

I shake my head and say "I'll be fine let's go sit and drink wine" she laughs, picks up the bottle of wine and follows me out to the conservatory where Luca and Uncle John are waiting.

We sit talking and drinking for a couple of hours, we do lots of laughing and my side is hurting a bit but I try not to show it. Aunty Susan and Uncle John go to bed and leave us downstairs to finish off the bottle of wine.

"Come here Kammie, come and sit on my lap, I need to feel you" Luca says, of course I do what he asks.

When I sit down, I look at him and he puts his hand behind my neck and gently brings me close to his face "I've wanted to do this all night" he says before he takes my lips in his and then plunges his tongue inside. I hear myself groan, I've wanted him to do that all night too.

His free hand rubs up and down my side very gently, it makes me feel warm and then he grabs my hip and pulls me closer. He groans "God Kammie, I thought you hated me when you ran, I need you so much I can't explain it." He turns me around so that I am straddling him and he rests his forehead on mine. "We are going to take this slow Kammie, neither of us wants to get scared by having a relationship, is that ok?

And no telling Tasha and Felix, we can ease them into the idea slowly when they get back from their honeymoon!"

He kisses me very gently on the lips and looks at me for a reaction. "I say that's a good plan Luca, now take me to bed" I say laughing.

All of a sudden he is really serious "Kammie I mean it, no sex straight away, this means too much already."

I start laughing "Luca I know, I'm joking, but really it's late and we have to drive home tomorrow. Anyway I wouldn't have sex in my Aunty's house" he smiles that devilish smile he has.

"Come on then teaser let's go" I get off his lap and take his hand to help pull him up, I wince a little and I know he sees me. He stands and pulls me close "I'm glad you came into my life Kammie, so glad."

I smile at him and take his hand and show him up to my room, we get undressed and climb into bed, he pulls me close and wraps one arm and leg around me. "This is my favourite position for sleeping Kammie."

I can feel myself falling asleep "Me too Luca, me too!"

13 Luca

I can't believe I am wrapped around Kammie again, I love being with her and I love sleeping with her. I really want to fuck her but I know we need to wait if we are going to make this relationship work. I really want this to work.

The last two days have been horrendous, when I woke up and she wasn't there I was disappointed, I thought she must have gone back to her room to freshen up. When she didn't come down for breakfast I started panicking thinking she was trying to avoid me. After I waited and then spoke to reception I thought she didn't want to see me again and that hurt like nothing has ever hurt before. What did I do to make her hate me? I went to her house and when I saw her car was gone I just thought she had gone out visiting family. I sat there all day waiting for her, I needed to know she didn't hate me.

I started to get worried that something had happened to her, then I wondered if she'd gone to see a guy or something. I sat outside her house all night, I'm surprised I wasn't arrested for being a stalker. I went to see Jean to see if she knew where she was, I know she could see I was worried so she rang Kammie's mum Brenda to find out. When she told me Kammie was in Torquay I didn't stop to think, I knew I just needed to get here and see her.

I walked up and down the beach for an hour before I saw her, then I just watched her for a while, she looked sad. I'm so glad I came here, she needed to understand how I feel.

I pull her in closer to me and totally wrap myself around her, I sigh and fall asleep.

When I wake in the morning, I'm sweating and then I realise that I'm totally wrapped up in Kammie and she is trying to move, I laugh "Good morning baby, did you sleep well?" I kiss her on the top of her head.

"Mmm" she says wriggling her fine ass up against my already hard cock!

I reach down and grab her ass "Baby stop! I want to fuck you so bad, that just makes it worse" she laughs.

"Luca I want you inside me making me squirm" she says seductively pushing up against me.

I reach across to the front of her body so quick I hear her take a sharp breath as my hand slips inside her panties. "Baby you are so wet and you feel so hot" I move my fingers up and down inside her lips. I tease the tip of my finger at her entrance, instinctively she opens her legs "Do you want my fingers inside you baby? Tell me what you want!" I stop moving my fingers waiting for her response.

"Luca don't stop, I want your fingers inside me, I want to know that you are going to lick them and taste them" she moans opening her legs further, god she is amazing, she's not afraid to tell me what she wants! I feel her hand on mine, she starts moving my fingers as if they are her own. God that's sexy she's using my fingers to masturbate with.

I groan, "Kammie you are going to be the death of me, you're so fucking sexy right now." I take control of my fingers and plunge them inside her hot core. I'm finding it really hard not to roll her over and fuck her till she cums.

I take them out and start rubbing her clit, she nudges my hand out the way so she can it rub herself "Put them inside Luca, please" I don't wait a second longer and I plunge 3 fingers inside. She is so wet and it isn't long before her walls clamp around my fingers and I can feel her body bucking against mine. She is trying so hard to stay quiet and I know she is finding it hard, she relaxes against my body and then she says "Luca let me taste your fingers" I really have died and gone to heaven with her. I move my fingers up her body and put them into her mouth, she groans, god I can't take this much longer.

All of a sudden, I don't know how it happened but she has pushed me back so that I am laying on my back, she crawls up my body until her mouth is level with my cock. She looks at me waiting for me to say its ok, she listened to what I told her about control in the bedroom. Fuck me she's amazing. She reaches out and touches my hard shaft and then leans her head down, slowly, too fucking slowly, and she licks the pre-cum off the tip, her mouth feels so hot, she opens her mouth wider. I can only stare at her with my mouth open copying hers.

She puts her mouth around the tip and slowly lowers her mouth over my cock until she has it all in her mouth. How the hell did she do that no one has ever taken it all like that. Her hands reach out and starts playing with my balls, she takes my cock out of her mouth and starts licking it like a lollipop, this makes me chuckle. "You find this funny do you?" She says as she holds the base of my cock and starts pumping it up and down, at the same time she takes it into her mouth and the sensation of the two together is too much, I take my fingers and taste them and smell them as I cum into her pretty mouth. All the time she is watching me and as I orgasm into her mouth I keep looking at her eyes, they are definitely the window to her soul.

"Luca you taste amazing" she says as she crawls up my body "here taste" she says as she plunges her tongue into my mouth.

We share an extremely passionate kiss and I already know that she is going to be the last person I ever kiss. After a few minutes she pulls away, smiles and then lowers herself so she is draped over my body with her head resting above my heart. My hand gently rubs her up and down on her back, this feels like heaven.

Kammie

Wow, just wow. That was the most emotional, passionate make out session I've ever had, Luca is definitely the one for me.

I can feel myself drifting off and then I remember where we are "Luca, we need to get up, I forgot where we are. We have to drive home today" I say sneaking a kiss and then rolling out of the bed. I get dressed and go downstairs to Aunty Susan who is laying the table for breakfast.

"Morning sweetie, did you sleep well?" she asks me.

I blush "Yes I did, so much better than the night before."

"I'm sure you did" she says smiling, I think I need to put her straight, I don't want her to think we were having sex in her house or anything. All of a sudden she starts laughing "Kammie, I know you wouldn't do anything in my house, I didn't mean that. I mean that after our chat the other night I know how much you care for Luca and it must have felt good to have him in your life again" she reaches forward and hugs me close to her.

"Aunty Susan, I can't even begin to explain to you how good it feels to have him here, for him to come all the way down here to find me, I won't ever forget that." I smile.

"He is worth everything Kammie, he wants you in his life and he won't let anything get in his way, just make sure it's what you want too."

"It is, he's the one I want" I can feel tears welling up in my eyes, this is momentous for me to have made a decision to be with Luca, in a relationship with Luca. I can't believe I've done that, I avoid relationships because I don't want the heartbreak!

"Let's get breakfast on the go" Aunty Susan says as she starts getting everything on the table.

"Morning girls!" I hear Luca say from outside the door, I wonder how much he heard, crap I don't want to scare him off.

"Morning Luca, did you sleep well" Aunty Susan says smiling at him.

"Yes I did thank you Susan, I just wanted to say thank you for welcoming me into your home and for looking after Kammie when she came to you" he comes over and takes my hand. I look at him and he smiles at me. Everything is going to be alright, I just know it.

After breakfast we get ready to head home, "Kammie, I don't want you to have to drive home, I'd rather be taking you home in my car with me."

"Luca, I need to bring my car, I have to get to work, I can't leave it here."

"I know Kammie, I just want to make sure you're ok and I want to spend the next 2 hours talking to you and not watching you drive home. I'm going to follow you though, is that ok?" he asks.

"Of course it is Luca, I'm a big girl and I can drive from here to Bristol you know" does he think I can't drive?

"Can I have 2 minutes with you outside please Kammie, I need to explain something to you" he says taking my hand and pulling me towards the back door.

"Luca what is it? What has got into you, of course I can drive home."

"Take a seat baby" he says bringing me out towards the garden seat. "I need to explain something to you and I don't want you to freak out or get upset"

He's worrying me now, but I nod for him to go on!

"Ok Kammie, I have feelings for you that I don't understand. Now that we agreed to take our friendship to another level, I can't let anything happen to you. I will do whatever it takes, within my control, to keep you safe. One of my best friends, other than Felix, decided to drive home from Newquay instead of coming with us and he crashed on the way home. I've always thought that I should have stopped him and made him come home with me, I can't lose you Kammie now that I have you in my life" he leans forward and kisses me.

"Luca that wasn't your fault and I'll be fine I'll drive 10mph if that's what you want. Honestly, I'll be ok" I hug him to me. I know how he feels I don't want to lose him either.

14 Luca

It's my birthday today and I can't wait to go out and party. Felix rang me during the week and told me he wasn't coming to Jesters tonight, it was a strange conversation because he likes to party just like me. Maybe he is trying to change now that he's married, he rang me last night to tell me that him and Tasha will be coming after all, I hope everything is ok, they both mean a lot to me.

I know Kammie is coming out tonight and I can't wait to see her again, I know it has only been a couple of days but I miss her laying next to me. Tonight is the night, tonight I am going to have sex with her, tonight I am going to let everyone know she is mine!

I take care getting ready, I want to make sure she wants me as bad as I want her. I meet Glen and we go to The Angel for a couple of drinks before we go to Jesters. It's packed in here and there are loads of willing young ladies, but there's only one girl for me. When we get to Jesters I see her waiting for me and I go over to her "Hey baby" I say coming up behind her and wrapping my arms around her stomach. I kiss her on her neck and whisper in her ear "Tonight I'm going to make you mine Kammie" I can feel her shiver.

"Really Luca, you think I want you tonight?" she says giggling. She knows what that does to me and I can feel her reaching behind her back with her hand and grabbing my growing cock. "Do you think I want this?" she tightens her grip, "I'll have to see if I have any better offers" she says letting go.

I can't take any more, I spin her around until she is facing me and I devour her mouth, she meets my tongue with her own and I can hear us both moaning, when I pull away I say "If you can get a better offer than that baby, work away" I walk away, I feel so horny I need to calm down.

As I'm walking over to the bar I see Kammie throwing herself at Tasha and I smile to myself, they are really good friends and it makes me happy to think that me and

Kammie are going to make a go of our relationship. I walk up to the bar and then Felix comes over to me and slaps me on my back to wish me a happy birthday. "Hey Luca, happy birthday mate, you old git."

I laugh at him, he is the same age as me "Takes one to know one Felix." He orders a couple of beers and we go into the private area I have booked for us all.

Felix looks towards the girls as Tasha signals that she is going dancing with Kammie, I can't take my eyes off Kammie she is so sexy tonight. I make sure wherever I am in Jesters that I can see her, I don't want to let her out of my sight.

I'm chatting to Felix when I see Tasha stumble and spill her drink all over some guy, she tries to wipe it up but he doesn't let her. I turn to Felix and tell him that she fell, maybe she is drunk and needs looking after so we both start to make our way over to the girls. I then see Tasha give the guy a piece of paper, I assume it is so that she can pay for his dry cleaning, I chuckle to myself. I stop and turn around to laugh with Felix about it and find he isn't there, I wonder where he is. I go and find him outside "Hey Felix what's going on? What are you doing outside?"

He looks really angry "Did you see what

was going on downstairs? We're only married a few weeks and she is already hitting on some bloke! What the fuck Luca?"

"Dude, listen to me she isn't hitting on someone, didn't you see her fall and spill her drink on him. Tasha is not the type of woman who cheats Felix, she was probably offering to pay for his dry cleaning. I don't know what's wrong with you this week, but you need to calm the fuck down!"

I turn and walk back inside and down to the dancefloor "Hey Kammie I was hoping for a birthday dance, come with me please?"

She turns to look at Tasha who smiles at her and then turns to me "Luca where's Felix?"

Shit I don't really want her to see him in his mood, maybe he has had too much to drink too. "I think he's outside he wasn't very happy, he looked really angry, so I think he went for some air. I don't know what made him like that, you know Felix he's usually so placid. It was strange!" I smile at Tasha and then Kammie drags me onto the dancefloor.

I forget all about Tasha as me and Kammie dance close together, anyone watching would know that this is foreplay, our bodies are getting to know each other before we explore them more indepth later.

I am lost in Kammie, her body, her lips "I can't wait to get you home later baby, I want you so bad." I look up and I notice Felix dragging Tasha at the side of the dance floor "What the fuck is going on?"

Kammie looks up at me and follows my line of sight "Luca, I don't like the look of that."

I take her hand and we walk over to Felix.

"Felix, what's going on? Where are you going? Any why are you dragging Tasha behind you like that?" I put my hand out to stop Felix, I don't think he is going to stop though.

He tells me to get out of the way, that he and Tasha need some alone time to discuss what happened tonight, he says that he needs to talk to her about giving another man her phone number. I have never seen Felix this angry before, I don't like the thought of him taking Tasha home in that mood.

"Come on mate, you don't need to talk to Tasha about that, she knows that and she would never do anything to make you think differently, what is really going on here?" I am getting really annoyed with Felix.

"Luca, just get out of my way or you might regret it. We've been friends for years and I intend for us to remain friends, but right now you need to let me go and take Tasha home." He's trying to get past me, but I'm not moving that easy.

"No Felix, you have to calm down right now, I am not letting you leave here in that mood and take Tasha home, I have never seen you like this, what has got into you?" I look at Tasha, "Tasha are you ok? What is going on?"

She starts to sob and all I want to do is to take hold of her and tell her everything is going to be ok. I can feel Kammie behind me trying to get past me, but I stop her. "Luca just let him past, please! Felix isn't happy because when he came to find me on the dance floor he saw me talking to a stranger who I had spilt my drink on when I tripped. Now he thinks I was up to something and I wasn't I swear."

I turn to Felix "Felix, this isn't you mate, come on calm down, please" I take my hand off him and he drags Tasha off again.

He stops and turns back to me "Luca, this doesn't have anything to do with you mate, please just leave it! I've calmed down but I just want to go home now it's been a long day. I'll ring you tomorrow ok? Maybe we can all do lunch or something."

Tasha says to me "Yeah Luca let's do lunch tomorrow, our treat, Kammie you come too, it will be nice," she smiles at me but I notice her smile doesn't reach her eyes.

I step out of the way as there is nothing else I can do, Felix says to me "Thanks Luca, me and my wife need some alone time" and then he walks away. I watch Tasha follow him out of Jesters and I signal for her to ring me if she needs anything.

When I turn around Kammie pulls me close and I can see she has tears in her eyes "Baby what is it?"

"Luca, what is wrong with Felix? I've never seen him like that. I hope everything is ok they've only been married a couple of weeks. This is why I don't do relationships, they have a habit of turning bad," she sniffs back her tears.

I hold her at arm's length and tuck her hair behind her ears, I take my thumb and rub away a lone tear which is breaking free, I kiss her on her eyes. "Baby, they are fine and don't dismiss our relationship before we have even begun, OK? We are not Felix and Tasha, we are Luca and Kammie and we will live our own life, not theirs".

She looks at me and doesn't say anything for a couple of minutes and then she kisses me and I can feel all her emotions in this kiss, this is her way of telling me that she won't dismiss us, that she does believe in us.

When she pulls away, I say "Come on let's go home, I want to make love to you and claim you as mine" she smiles at me and takes my hand. We say goodbye to the others and leave Jesters.

We jump into a cab and go back to my apartment, as soon as we are in the house, I push her up against the door and devour her mouth. Our tongues clash in our haste to taste each other.

Kammie

Tonight has been a rollercoaster of emotions, I was concentrating on Luca and trying to get him horny because when he told me tonight was the night I was so excited. I wasn't really watching Tasha, she seemed to be enjoying herself so I didn't think anything of it, but seeing the way Felix was with her upset me more than I can even begin to explain.

It was the way she reacted so calmly, not answering him back, I would have told him to fuck off and leave me alone, but she told Luca she was going to be fine. What has been going on and what have I missed? I'm glad we are getting together on Tuesday because we really need to talk.

When we get back to Luca's house he pushes me up against the door and devours me. I love him when he's being controlling, it really turns me on.

As he takes my hand to lead me upstairs his phone rings, he looks at me and then at the screen "It's Felix" he says, I know he needs to take it especially after earlier, I nod for him to take the call.

Felix is shouting so I can hear him, he sounds hysterical "Luca, it's Tasha, please come to the house, please come she fell down the stairs and she needs help." I try to let go of Luca's hand but he won't let me, he pins me with a stare.

"Felix you need to get an ambulance, I can't help her." Luca is starting to get annoyed, but I can see he is worried too.

"No, I'm not calling an ambulance, she'll be ok, just come round and tell me what to do." I can hear Felix and he is getting more desperate.

"Ok Felix, I'm coming round, Kammie is here with me and I'll bring her too, don't do anything stupid." He hangs up the phone and we walk back down the stairs.

"Luca what happened? Do you think he did something to her, he was mad enough earlier, I hope she'll be ok." I start sobbing, she's my friend, my sister and I don't want anything to have happened to her.

"Come on Kammie, you need to be strong for Tasha, she might need a friend when we get there. Come on baby" he has me pulled in tight to his body and he's not letting me go. "She'll be fine, I promise, she probably just slipped, you saw how drunk she was" I nod.

He rings for a taxi because we have had too much to drink, although I feel sober enough to drive. The taxi comes really quickly and we slide into the back of it, this journey isn't like the one we had earlier where we couldn't keep our hands off each other. Luca pulls me closer to him and puts his arm around my shoulders, he keeps kissing me on the side of my head "Baby it'll be fine." I'm not sure who he is trying to convince - me or himself. We are quiet for the rest of the journey and we almost jump out when we arrive at Tasha's house.

15 Luca

We arrive at Felix's house after a quiet journey, I don't know what to expect, I'm sure Felix is just being a drama queen, Tasha just slipped and she's fine now, probably just a little bruised but fine. That's what I'm hoping anyway, I want to go home and claim my birthday present. I look at Kammie and I can see she is really worried, I pull her close to me as we walk to the front door, I have my arm around her shoulder and then I drop it to hold her hand. She looks at me and she looks like a frightened child, in that moment I know I am falling in love with her, I want to protect her from whatever is on the other side of the door. This doesn't frighten me as much as I thought it would, that is because it is

Kammie and she is the right person for me, she is my other half!

I shake my head because I need to concentrate on Felix and Tasha, I kiss Kammie briefly on her lips, "Come on baby let's go and see what all the fuss is about, but you are coming back to mine tonight, I need to protect you and look after you" she smiles at me and everything feels alright.

I turn and open the front door which is unlocked. What I see frightens me and I pull Kammie behind me so that she can't see immediately, I know that is the wrong thing to do to her because she steps out so that she can see perfectly. Tasha is laid at the bottom of the stairs, she is at a funny angle, she has a lump on the side of her head, but what frightens me most is that she has red marks around her neck, there is no way they got there from falling down the stairs. I can feel bile rising into my mouth and I have to swallow it down because I need to be strong for everyone in the room.

Kammie goes and kneels down at Tasha's side "Tasha, please speak to me, come on I don't know what's happened here and to be honest I don't care. But what I do need is for you to be ok, come on Tasha, please."

My heart breaks for her. "Felix. She. Will. Die. If you don't get her help" I am getting really angry now at Felix.

"OK, OK can you ring them? I just can't do it, I'm scared Luca" he's obviously lost his balls.

I ring 112 and tell them what happened and they say that an ambulance is on the way. The few minutes it takes feels like a year, none of us say a word, we just all sit looking at Tasha making sure she is still breathing. We are scared to move her because her neck looks like it is broken or something, it is at a strange angle.

When the ambulance arrives, they immediately put her onto a trolley and take her to hospital, Felix goes in the back with her, I walk out with him. "Felix, me and Kammie will clear up here and close the house up, we will come to the hospital to find you. Make sure you keep me up to date with everything that is happening, please Felix." He nods at me as he is so emotional he is unable to speak.

I stand there and watch the ambulance drive off, I ring for a taxi to come and collect us and take us to the hospital. It's another few minutes before I compose myself enough to go back in the house to Kammie, who is sitting on the bottom step waiting for me.

I go and sit next to her "Are you OK Kammie?" I put my arm around her and pull her close, she rests her head on my shoulder.

"Not really Luca, I'm worried about Tasha, what the hell happened in here? Did she really fall down the stairs Luca? You saw how angry Felix was, could he have pushed her? I can't even begin to think that he could do that to her, he loves her."

"Kammie, he loves her so much he wouldn't do that to her. Tasha would have said something if he didn't, come on I called a taxi to take us to the hospital because I think we both need to see that she is ok." I stand and hold my hand out to her to help her up, she takes it and I pull her close into a hug. "Baby we are doing this together, you are not on your own here, I'm not going anywhere remember that" I kiss the top of her head.

"Thanks Luca it means so much to me to have you in my life." She's all muffled because her head is against my chest.

I lead her outside to wait for the taxi and I turn the lights off and lock the door, we sit on the top step for about 5 minutes and then the taxi arrives.

Kammie

We get in the taxi and I look back at Tasha's house as we drive away, it's in the dark and it looks gloomy or maybe that's just my mood.

Luca holds my hand and we don't really say very much. We get to the hospital and find Felix, they are moving her into a room of her own, so we follow them down. She's in and out of consciousness, when we get to her room the doctor stops me and Luca from going in. "I'm sorry immediate relatives only, she needs to be examined and then she needs rest." He's very nice, but he's pissing me off.

"That's my best friend in there, I want to know how she is and what's happened to her." I start shouting because I'm frustrated he won't let me see her.

"Kammie he's only doing his job, Tasha's health has to come first here. We can sit and wait out here until there's any news. I'll go get us some coffees in the meantime." Luca is trying to keep me calm, I nod my head and he leaves me. Before I take a seat I walk up to the door and beckon Felix to come out to me.

He looks at me and comes over to the door "What is it Kammie?"

"Come out here for a minute I want to talk to you Felix" I say calmly.

He comes out of the room and closes the door gently.

"What happened Felix? What really happened? Is she going to be alright?" I'm still calm but all I want to do is shake him to tell me what happened.

"Kammie we were arguing about the guy in Jesters, she stormed off to go downstairs and get a drink to take her headache tablets and she tripped and fell down the stairs. I ran down as fast as I could after her, but she didn't respond, so I rang Luca and you know the rest."

"I know how angry you were Felix, you must have been having some row for her to be going fast down the stairs when she had been drinking. Why didn't you just ring the ambulance? Why did you call Luca and then wait for him to ring them? I don't understand that part." I'm shaking my head as I'm pacing up and down.

"Kammie, everything happened so quick and I panicked, I thought she was fine but I knew she was hurt. I don't know why I rang Luca instead of an ambulance but everything is going to be fine now. I promise." He reaches out to touch me on my shoulder and I flinch and keep pacing.

"I hope for your sake she is fine Felix, because so help me god if she's not." I start to get angry and then I feel a hand on my shoulder that instantly calms me down, it's Luca.

"Come on Kammie, Felix has had a shock too, let's sit down and wait to see if we can go in to see Tasha." He says guiding me over to the seats, I watch Felix as he walks back into the room looking sad and down to the ground.

I sit and Luca hands me my coffee, I wrap my hands around it and take a sip. We are both quiet for a while then Luca takes my hand "I'll go check if we can see her, if not then we might as well go home. Are you coming back to mine, I don't want you to be on your own tonight baby you've had a shock" he lifts my hand and kisses it.

I sigh, "I'd love to come back to yours Luca, I don't want to be on my own and it's still your birthday." I smile at him.

He smiles back and stands to go and see if we can see Tasha. After a few minutes he comes back shaking his head so I stand and he puts his arm around my shoulder and pulls me in tight "Come on baby let's go home," it sounds so good when he says that, it's like I belong there with him.

When we get back to his house, Luca takes my hand and pulls me upstairs, "Kammie I don't know if we should have sex tonight, with everything that's gone on it doesn't seem right, I want our first time to be special."

I don't have to think about what he says, I know he's right "I feel the same way Luca but I do want you to hold me all night, please."

"That goes without saying baby, I love having you laid in my bed as close as you can get" he pushes me up against the wall in his bedroom and kisses me like it's the last time he will see me. "You make me feel things I've never felt before Kammie, I like these feelings but I'm trying to get used to them. I want you so much but I want what we have to mean more than sex."

"I feel the same way Luca, I want you like I've never wanted anyone before, you make me feel like I'm a virgin who needs to be treated delicately, I like that." I kiss him and then he pulls me to the bed and slowly takes my clothes off.

"You don't need to wear anything in bed baby, I need you to be as close as you can."

I smile at him when he starts to take all his clothes off too, god he has an amazing body. We get under the covers and I roll onto my side facing him, I trace his tattoos, they are beautiful. "I'll tell you the story behind them all one day baby, it's too late right now" I roll back over and he pulls me next to him, he puts his leg over me and then his arm, this is home!

16 Luca

I woke up this morning with a raging hard on, it takes me a minute to realise that Kammie is under the covers with my cock in her mouth. Wow that is hot! I slowly lift the covers and I see her eyes lift to look up at me, she smiles while she has her mouth full, then she reaches out and takes hold of the base of my cock and slowly takes it out of her mouth. "Morning Luca, hope you didn't mind, you were stabbing me when I woke up so I thought I'd help you out" she giggles, I lay my head back down because that giggle is going to be my undoing. I throw the covers off us so that I can see her, it is such a turn on to see my cock going in and out of her mouth, I'm trying to hold on because I want to watch her, she looks like she's eating a lollipop licking it, sucking it then moving it around with her tongue when it's in her mouth.

"Baby I don't know if I can hold on you'd better take it out of your mouth or I'll cum in your mouth." Her eyes light up and she reaches down to play with my balls, then she starts running her finger between my balls and my ass, oh my god that has me spurting my hot cum into her mouth before she can move an inch. She takes it all, her eyes watching me all the time, she swallows it all, gulp gulp gulp.

When I've finished she takes it out of her mouth and licks me clean, then she slowly crawls up my body and straddles me and leans forward and kisses me, hard. "Morning Luca you taste great mmm I enjoyed my breakfast." She smiles at me and I can't believe how lucky I am, she is beautiful, funny and very loving, I'm so lucky.

I put my hands on her ass and rub her over my cock, it feels so good, hot and wet, god she's wet. When she least expects it I roll her over so I'm on top and I take her legs and open them wider than they were, I kneel and put her legs over my shoulders, she looks at me with wide open eyes. "It's my breakfast time now Kammie and you are on my menu." She giggles, I lean down and plunge my tongue between her lips, she gasps, I look at her over the top of her mound, her eyes are still open wide. I move my hand down to her lips and slowly plunge my finger inside her, she is so wet.

I flick my tongue over her clit gently, I take my finger out and plunge two fingers in then I turn my hand so that when I make a beckoning motion with my fingers I touch her fleshy nub. She starts to wriggle and giggle, "Luca god that feels amazing, keep doing that, lick me harder please." I do as she asks, it doesn't take her long before she is pushing herself closer to my face as she screams my name out into the quiet of the room, she is sweating.

I smile and lick her clean, then I gently let her legs down off my shoulders and kiss her gently on her hips, then move up her body and take one of her nipples into my mouth, she squirms under me. I move up until I get to her beautiful face and I devour her mouth. When I pull away I smile and say "Good morning baby, that was a great way to wake up, thank you. Now how about a shower and then a proper breakfast" she smiles at me and nods her head. We climb out of bed and jump into the shower, where we clean each other down and then when we are dressed we go downstairs.

While we are having coffee and chatting about last night Felix rings. "Hey Luca, I'm on my way to see Tasha and wanted to ask if you and Kammie would come over for dinner this evening, I'll cook. I'm sure she will be getting out today, but if there's a change in plan I'll let you know. Can you contact Kammie and ask her too?"

"Hey yeah I'll come over, I'll have to ask Kammie though, I know she was angry with you last night, but I'm sure she will do it for Tasha." Kammie is looking at me, she heard me talking about her. "Any news on Tasha?"

"I rang and they said she had a comfortable night, the doctor will be going around in an hour or so and he will let us know if she can go home. Thanks Luca for last night and for coming over for dinner tonight."

"No worries Felix, see you later, let us know if there's any news." I hang up my phone and look at Kammie who is just staring at me wanting to know what was said.

"Felix is on his way over to see Tasha, he doesn't really have any news except that he is hoping she will be home this evening, he wants us to go for dinner like he said last night. Are you ok with that baby?" I don't know how she will react.

"Luca I don't think I'm comfortable being in Felix's company, I just want to shout at him for not taking control last night, he shouldn't have called you and expected you to go over and clean up his mess" she is getting really angry again.

I stand up and go and stand behind her, I bend over and hug her from behind "Kammie, at least he told someone, what if he had just left her? Did you think about that? What would have happened to her if she just stayed at the bottom of the stairs for the night?" I kiss her on her neck slowly, up towards her ear, I know she likes that. I am starting to know her body and her responses to me, I like that. I've never been with anyone long enough to know what they like only what women like in general. She starts reacting to me by calming down and then I hear her sigh.

"I know you're right Luca, I'm sorry and of course I'll go to dinner. I want to know how Tasha is and I want to make sure that she is ok with Felix" she leans back into my neck and I kiss her again at the base of her neck.

"I'll be with you Kammie, we will be going together and then you can come back to mine or we can go back to yours after, I'm not leaving you alone tonight baby." I want to tell her that I don't want to ever leave her alone ever again, but I don't want to scare her.

Kammie

After breakfast I went home to get changed and to have a couple of hours on my own. I needed time to think, things with Luca have moved very quickly in a small space of time and I needed to re-evaluate. Before I chilled out I got changed and went to the hospital, I had to see Tasha and see she was alright. I asked her what happened and she said that she fell down the stairs, I'm not sure I believe her but she is my best friend, why would she lie to me? We arrange to meet at Tasha's house and I go back home.

While I'm at home I think about Tasha and what happened last night, she was drunk so she probably did slip down the stairs, Felix wouldn't really push her down the stairs, he loves her too much.

I also think about Luca, he is so wonderful and everything I ever wanted, but I know that we are both not used to relationships so I understand that he wants to take things slowly. I wish he'd have sex with me though, I can feel the sexual tension coming off the two of us and I know it will be explosive when we finally do have sex.

Luca comes by to pick me up so that we can go to Tasha's together, I like that it makes us feel like more than just friends. I open the door and ask him to come in. "Hey, I'm nearly ready come in!"

He comes through my door and then he grabs me by my waist and pulls me close to him. "Can I have a proper hello? Come here" he kisses me hard, like he hasn't seen me for a long time. It feels good, it feels right!

When he pulls away he smiles at me "Hey baby, that's better" he takes my hand and leads me into the lounge. I'm just able to close the front door behind me. "So what did you do when you came home? Did you rest? I was so tired, it was a long night but a fantastic morning" he smiles and it goes all the way to his eyes.

"I went to the hospital to see Tasha" he raises his eyebrows. "I needed to see for myself that she was OK" I look down to the ground and sigh.

"How was she? Is she coming home today?" he asks leading me to the couch to sit down.

"She was ok, she said that she had fallen

down the stairs because she was in a rush to get downstairs to get a drink, I'm not sure I believe her but at the same time I have to believe her because she is my friend."

"I think we have to believe her Kammie, if there was something happening she had the opportunity to tell you and she didn't so we can just believe her, but we can keep an eye on her too! I agreed with Felix that I will look after her for the next couple of days and make sure she is ok, that was the only way the doctor was going to let her come home." Luca says, he has his arm behind me on the couch and all the time he was talking he was twisting a piece of my hair around his finger.

"I think you're right Luca, come on then let's go and see what Felix can cook up." I smile at him and he leans forward and presses a gentle kiss on my lips. I like the feelings he is evoking in me.

We stand up and Luca automatically takes my hand, like he isn't even thinking about it, I like that!

After I lock the front door, I climb into his car and he closes the door and then goes around to the other side to get inside himself.

We talk about the party last night before everything happened, I think we've all forgotten it was his birthday, I feel sorry for him, I'll have to make it up another time. I can think of plenty of things to make him smile.

When we pull up to their house Luca parks the car, he turns to me and says "Come on lets go and see Tasha, I'm coming back to yours tonight, I don't want you to be on your own" he winks at me, I smile back at him.

"How can I say no to you Luca?" I laugh, we both get out of the car laughing and walk up to the front door. I have a key and I just let us in, I've always done that.

Luca walks through to Felix who is in the kitchen and I walk into the lounge and see Tasha sleeping on the couch. I stand looking at her for a few minutes and I can feel the tears welling up in my eyes, I kneel in front of her and she wakes up. "Hi sleepyhead, how are you feeling?" I ask.

She smiles at me "I feel fine Kammie it's just a bit sore when I laugh so don't make any jokes at dinner time"

I smile at her because she always makes jokes "OK fine I promise" I hold out my hand to help her up.

We walk to the kitchen linking arms,

Luca goes over and hugs Tasha very gently like she is bone china and he doesn't want to break her.

When we walk into the kitchen the smell hits me, it smells delicious "Dinner's going to be 10 minutes" Felix says "Why don't you take a seat and relax" he says to Tasha, he really loves her a lot.

We all enjoy dinner, Felix made Roast Beef and it was delicious, we had wine with the meal, Luca only had one because he is driving tonight. Tasha asks us whether we think she should go to her interview in the morning, we all said that she was the only one who could make that decision. We chat for a while and have a very pleasant evening.

Luca says "OK, well I'm on duty tomorrow morning so I'll come over early and I can drive you to the interview if you want to go, if not then we can just hang here. OK Tasha?" She nods at him and then we both get up on and go into the lounge while the boys clean up the kitchen.

Tasha tells me about the interviews she has lined up and they both sound exciting, I know she will go to the interviews because she really wants a new job. She starts to get tired and when the boys come into the lounge she says she wants to go to bed.

Luca tells her he will be over early and he will take her if she wants to go.

Before she goes upstairs, she kisses Felix goodnight and they look so happy and they are so well suited, it puts a smile on my face.

We all watch her walking up the stairs and then we say goodbye to Felix "I'll see you in the morning Felix" Luca says. "Hope Tasha sleeps ok tonight" he slaps him on the shoulder.

I go over to Felix and give him a hug "Night Felix, if you need anything you know where we are" he hugs me back.

We walk out to Luca's car and then we drive to my house, I'm glad Luca said he was going to stay the night I could do with someone to talk to. Who am I kidding? I just want him in my bed!

17 Luca

We were quiet on the way home, but I was happy that everything was ok with Felix and Tasha, Kammie should be happy too. I don't want this weekend to end, it's been a very strange one, but it's been amazing at the same time. I have found something this weekend that I never thought I would find. It scares me but at the same time I can't wait to embrace it.

When we get inside Kammie's house, I can't hold back so I push her against the wall and take her hands and raise them above her head, I hold them tight with one of my hands and I use the other one to very slightly touch her body while I kiss her delectable mouth.

I run my fingertips down the outside of

TO HAVE AND TO HOLD

her breasts and then down her body, she can barely feel it but she knows what I am doing. I pull away only slightly and whisper in her ear "Baby I want you so much" I run my hand around to the small of her back and then I pull her so that she is closer to me and can feel the length of my cock. "Can you feel how much I want you Kammie?" she nods her head, unable to speak. "Let's go upstairs" I say to her, letting go of her hands and bringing them around to her back, I continue to hold them together and she walks up the stairs in front of me.

This turns me on, this is what I like, to have complete control over a woman, to give her so much pleasure that she is begging me to let her cum. The feeling I have with Kammie in this position is intensified because I know I have strong feelings for her and I know that she feels the same way. I wonder what it is going to feel like to make love to her, I want to fuck her, but first I want to love her.

When we get into her bedroom, I slowly peel her clothes off, she is still facing away from me, but she lets me take her clothes off and she doesn't turn around to face me, she wants me to show her what I like so that she can see if she likes it too. This is an important moment for both of us, I don't want to frighten her away and I know she wants to enjoy this too. "Kammie you are so beautiful" I say kissing down her spine as she stands facing the bed. "The things I want to do to you." I kiss over the cheeks of her ass – I still have hold of her hands, they just touch the top of her ass cheeks – my other hand caresses around the front of her body and stops just between her legs.

"Luca please touch me, please" she's begging me, I love the sound of a woman begging. I slowly run my fingertips up the inside of her thigh as slow as I can, teasing with every little touch. As I get closer to her core I lick and then kiss her ass, I can feel her goose bumps growing as she gets excited by my touch. I nip her between my teeth in the crook of her ass, she instantly groans "Luca please."

I slowly stand up and push her towards the bed very gently "I want you to lay down Kammie, face down with your hands stretched out above your head – will you do that for me?"

She nods her head "Talk to me Kammie, this doesn't work unless you keep talking to me"

"Yes Luca I'll do that for you" she says as she starts to lower herself down onto the bed. I watch her as she does what I asked and she looks so beautiful face down on her bed with her arms above her head. I quickly take my own clothes off, I need to feel her naked body against my own.

"Now baby, I am going to take this slow, very slow and I need you to tell me if you don't like something ok? I also need you to hold on and not cum until I'm ready for you to cum – can you do that baby?" I've knelt at the bottom of the bed.

"Luca, just carry on – I'm ready for you and whatever you want to do" god she turns me on so much.

I spread her legs open, I can see her very slightly lift her ass, she doesn't know what to expect from me but she is ready whatever I want to do. I lean forward and kiss gently along the inner side of her thigh up towards her very core, I hear her gasp and hold her breath, she is waiting for me to touch her between her legs. I smile because I know I won't be doing that just yet!

I spread her legs, she lifts her ass and I kiss my way down her leg and then back up again, I can't wait any longer I have to taste her. When I reach the top of her legs I very slowly pull her lips apart and stick the tip of my tongue in between them. I hear her moan, she lifts her ass even further like an invitation for me to plunge my cock in between them.

I plunge my tongue inside her hot channel and she wriggles her ass so that she can get closer and I can go deeper. She moans, I moan and then I pull my tongue out and I lick down to her clit which I then flick and she starts to giggle. "Luca that really tickles, please you have to fuck me I need you inside me, please"

I want to make this last for a lot longer, but I can't deny her what she wants so badly. I hold my cock with my hand and when I pull my mouth away I raise myself up and slowly guide my cock to her entrance. "Luca" she says and I can hear she is getting impatient but she still isn't moving, she's waiting for me to make the first move.

"Kammie I'm going to give you what you want, but only because I want it to." I carefully and slowly put the tip of my cock inside her, she holds her breath as she waits for me to push it all the way in. I do what she wants.

"Oh my god Luca, please" she is panting, I have to hold still, I am so turned on – I have never been this turned on in my life, it is an amazing feeling being inside Kammie, it is like we are meant to be together. It's not enough I need to see her beautiful face, I pull out – she groans, "No way Luca put it back" I flip her over so that I can see her, so that she can see me and then I push her up the bed and open her legs wide. I line myself up and then plunge my cock inside once more.

I stop and look at her face, she is so beautiful and I see tears coming out of her eyes. "Baby what's wrong, don't you want this? I'll stop if you want me to. Don't cry please" I wipe the tears away with my thumb.

"Luca please don't stop, I want this more than I've ever wanted anything, I just feel overwhelmed that's all, please Luca" she looks at her arms which are still above her head, she hadn't moved them because I hadn't told her she could. I nod to let her know she can move them and she moves them down my body and soon she puts them on my ass. I can feel her nails digging into my soft flesh as she pulls me as close as I can get.

I move slowly because I want to love her, I don't want to fuck her tonight I want to make love to her. I kiss her nipples and take her breast into my mouth as I slowly gyrate my hips and pull out and push it back in. I can feel my tension building, I don't know if I can last much longer "Baby I'm getting close, do you want your release? Do you need it too?"

"Yes Luca please let me cum, I need to

cum so bad it's killing me." She digs her nails into my ass and pulls me in close, I can feel her hands moving around to the front as she grabs my balls I start to speed up, I need my release, I pound my cock inside her and I can feel her start to swell inside and clamp around my cock as she screams out my name! "Luca oh my god Luca."

To hear those words coming out of her mouth at this moment in time sends me spiralling out of control, I pound her two more times and then I hold still while my hot cum spurts inside her. I look into her eyes and she looks into mine at the same time, I can feel the emotion passing between us and I flop on top of her, she wraps her arms and legs around me, pulling me close. "Kammie you are amazing, that was unbelievable, I never knew I could feel so many emotions all at once." I kiss her on the nape of her neck and she moans.

"Fuck Luca that was out of this world, I knew you'd be good but fuck me I want to do it again." She says and I start laughing, she starts laughing and then we roll onto our sides facing each other. I run my finger over her face and keep placing small kisses all over, she is so beautiful. She starts to snuggle down into me, but I need to pull out – I don't want to, I want to stay buried inside her for ever.

"Baby I need to go clean up, stay where you are and don't move" she smiles at me as I slowly pull out and disappear into the bathroom. I clean myself up and then bring out a facecloth soaked in warm water and start to clean her between her legs. She looks startled "Has no one ever done this to you Kammie? You need to be looked after just like a princess." I take the cloth once she is clean and wash it out and then I climb back into the bed – she has pulled the covers up over herself and is waiting for me.

I lay on my side and she snuggles backwards until she fits perfectly, I wrap my arm and my leg over her and then I kiss her on the nape of her neck. "Night baby, I'm going to keep you safe." I can already feel her body relaxing as she starts to fall asleep. I lay in the dark thinking about my life and how much better it feels for having Kammie in it. I pull her close and fall asleep with a smile on my face.

Kammie

When I wake up I know I have a smile on my face! I roll over onto my back and put my arms out and realise that I am able to stretch out in the bed, that means that Luca isn't there. I roll over to his side of the bed and it still feels warm so it means he hasn't been gone long. I feel disappointed because I thought after last night he wouldn't just sneak away like a thief in the night, I thought we had something special last night. I can feel myself getting upset and then I hear a noise, I realise it's the shower and it's turned on. I smile and quietly get out of bed and sneak into the bathroom. He hasn't heard me so I open the shower door and climb in next to him "Morning Luca, having a shower without me?"

"Well I was" he says pulling me close and kissing me "but this is much more enjoyable." He takes the body wash and starts to rub it on my body, I could get used to this.

"I thought you'd snuck away without saying goodbye" I say pouting, it's really hard though because he is rubbing the body wash over my breasts.

"Why would I do that baby? We are more than that – you know that" he kisses me again. His hand reaches down my stomach and he continues to wash me, he then bends and washes my legs all the way up to the top. When he reaches the top of my legs he slowly plants a kiss on my sweet spot and looks up at me. I smile and then he slowly kisses up my body until he reaches my mouth. He then devours my mouth, pushes me against the wall and plunges his tongue inside, when he pulls it out he says "I'm sorry baby but I have to go and meet Tasha, we can finish this off later."

I sigh because I am slightly disappointed, but he's right I have to go to work anyway. I nod my head and then he steps out of the shower, I wash my hair and then step out too. He has dried himself off and he is standing there with my towel open for me. I step into it and he embraces me, closing the towel around me as he does it.

He starts to rub me all over to dry me off. "Luca you really need to stop doing that if you want to get out of here in time to meet Tasha, because right now I just want to push you on the floor and fuck you senseless." He stops what he is doing and then looks at me with surprise in his eyes.

He starts to laugh "Baby you never cease to surprise me, those nasty words out of your lips are so fucking gorgeous and they are turning me on, but I really need to go." He steps back and I can see how much he is turned on, his tent is standing proud.

I kiss him on the lips and then turn to get my makeup on, he leaves the bathroom, laughing as he goes and gets dressed. When I'm finished in the bathroom I go into the bedroom and get changed, again he's disappeared! When I go downstairs I find him in the kitchen with a cup of coffee for me and a huge smile on his face.

"I have to go but I hope you have a good day and think about me, will I see you tonight baby?" He says kissing me just under my ear on my neck.

"Mmm if you promise to do that then yes most definitely," he laughs and it sends vibrations down my body. "Now get out and go look after my friend."

He stands up straight and puts two fingers against his head in salute "yes boss" he says smiling at me. He leans forward and kisses me deeply "See you later, have a good day at work" and then he leaves.

When I've heard the door close I lean against the kitchen counter and sigh, I don't know what is happening between us and I don't know where it will go but I like it already, I like it a lot! I take a deep breath, finish my coffee and then leave to go to work. I have a lot of gossip to talk to Jenny about today. I smile all the way to work.

As soon as I get in the office, Jenny comes to see me "What has put that smile on your face? It has to be a man, it is isn't it? Tell me all the details, I need to hear them" she doesn't stop for a breath.

I laugh "Jenny let's do lunch and then I'll tell you all the details ok."

"OK spoilsport I needed something to get me through a dreary Monday morning, you usually give me something to think about" she walks off towards her desk chuckling.

At lunchtime we go over to the park near the office, with our sandwich that we picked up on the way. We sit on the wall and neither of us says anything, we are both really hungry. Once the sandwiches are out of the way Jenny looks at me and says "So .... come on spill the beans, I can tell this one is different" she smiles.

She knows me too well "Well do you remember I told you about Luca, Tasha's friend? Well we kind of got together, I don't know what's happening between us but I know it's nothing like anything I have ever experienced before Jenny. It feels fan-bloody-tastic but it also feels strange, I want to text him, I want to ring him and I'm not like that. I'm so trying not to contact him, but I really want to. Does that make sense?"

Jenny laughs at me "Yes Kammie that is

how most of us feel when we meet someone who might be special to us, you've just never done it before. You always go for the easy option of one night stands, you never see someone twice, so of course it feels different. You want to see Luca and right now you are panicking internally that he isn't thinking about you and he doesn't want to see you again. Welcome to my world – at last" she says holding her hand up for a high five!

I give her a high five and the two of us sit around laughing for the rest of our lunch hour. I don't tell her any specifics of what happened between me and Luca because I don't know if I understand myself what happened and where it is heading. As I'm going back to work my phone beeps with a text, it's Luca:

Hey just wanted to see how you are, things are not the best here, will explain another time but just wanted to say hi xx

He even put a kiss at the end, I wonder what he means about things not being the best.

Hi. Is Tasha OK? Did she not go for her interview?

She's fine and yes she did go to her interview. We are watching films at the moment and she has fallen asleep. I was thinking about you baby and I wanted you to know xx

Phew thank god she's ok. I was thinking about you too and I'm on my way back to work, you just caught me. See you later?

Try and stop me, just try xx

I know I have a goofy smile on my face when Jenny says "Oh my god, was that him, you have it bad girl, real bad!"

I just laugh, but I think she's right!

The rest of the day passes in a flurry of admin work and meetings, soon enough it's time to go home and I don't know whether to go to my house or back to Luca's. This is what I don't like about relationships, that you are supposed to know these things. I laugh to myself – am I really stressing about where I will see Luca tonight?

As I'm driving home my phone rings, I glance at the phone and my heartbeat picks up and sees that it is Luca.

"Hey are you finished work? I could really do with having a couple of drinks tonight."

Oh here it comes, he doesn't want to see

me!

"Can we go out to dinner or something? I'd like to have some food and a few drinks, I know it's a school night but I just need to relax."

Phew, thank god I was wrong.

"Of course we can, or if you want I can cook dinner and we can have some wine! Your choice Luca"

"Well then I think I prefer the idea of staying in and cooking, will I go and buy some stuff and then come over to yours?"

"Yeah do that and bring your stuff for staying over too"

"I'm liking that idea a lot baby, see you in about an hour, drive carefully."

"See you soon Luca!"

I look in my rear view mirror and see a huge smile looking at me, it's me – I feel happy.

I get stuck in traffic so when I get home Luca is sitting on my doorstep waiting for me. I get out of the car and he stands up.

"I hope you weren't waiting long for me."

"Only about 10 minutes, I got everything together quicker than I thought." He comes towards me and leans down and I can feel my heartbeat speeding up and then it stops as he kisses me on the lips. It's a slow, sensual kiss and it literally takes my breath away.

When he pulls back I just stand there looking at him, I don't know what to say. Within seconds I come back down to reality and realise he is looking at me and it's then I notice he still has the grocery bags in his hands.

"Sorry Luca, let me open the door" I walk past him and open the front door, he goes in first and puts the groceries in the kitchen, then he comes out and picks up his overnight bag that he had left on the step.

When he has everything in I close the front door, he pushes me against it and says "Can I have a proper kiss now –I've been waiting all day for it." Without waiting for me to answer he takes my two hands and lifts them above my head, then he holds them together with one of his hands and with his free hand he runs his fingertip down my face. "Hey beautiful" he rests his finger under my chin and pushes it up so that I have to look into his eyes, his mouth crashes down onto mine so quickly I didn't see it coming.

He kisses me with so much passion it makes me want to cry, I'm not used to kissing someone and it meaning anything other than a prelude to sex. I feel myself melt into him and he runs his finger down the outside of my breasts and then around to the small of my back. He pulls away slightly and says "God I needed you today" into my mouth and then kisses me again.

When he finally pulls away he puts a small peck on my lips and then brings my arms slowly down and then takes one of my hands, "Come on I'll cook" he says pulling me gently to the kitchen. I can't do anything else but follow him.

He pulls out the chair for me to sit down and then he opens a bottle of wine and pours me a glass. "Now you sit there and watch me cook you up something nice" he kisses me on the nose and then turns to start cooking.

18 Luca

As I'm making dinner my mind is in turmoil after Tasha's revelation today that this wasn't the first time Felix had hurt her. She made me promise I wouldn't say anything to Felix or anyone else and it's killing me because I really want to make a go of my relationship with Kammie and don't want to start by lying to her.

"Are you ok Luca?" she says coming up behind me and wrapping her arms around me.

I slowly turn around into her arms "Yeah I'm fine, I was just thinking about Tasha we had a good day today, but I could see she was in pain, I think she thought she could hide it but she didn't."

"Tasha is strong and determined Luca she'll be fine. Did she say anymore about Saturday night?"

"Not really, I think she was trying to avoid it." I need to change the subject. "Anyway tell me about work today, anything exciting happen?" I smile and move out of her arms to continue cooking dinner.

"No I went to lunch with Jenny and we had a laugh, it was nice."

I nod my head and then she starts laying the table for dinner. We chat about our jobs and Kammie tells me about the films she is going to watch with Tasha later in the week when it is her turn to look after her.

After dinner we go into the lounge and watch a film on the TV, this has become so comfortable so quickly and, if I'm honest, it is a little scary, but it also feels like I've come home. I pull Kammie closer, I feel like I need to be as close to her as possible.

When it's time for bed, I hold out my hand for her to take and I gently pull her up the stairs. We get undressed, all the time watching each other, waiting to see what happens next.

We both get into the bed and she rolls onto her side and I pull her into me, "I love you being in that position baby," she giggles. "Do you know when you giggle it gets me hard? Every damn time!" I groan into her neck.

She giggles again "Oh I see what you mean" she wriggles against my cock.

Before she can stop me, I have slid myself inside her. She feels hot and she is already wet. I take my time, making love to her like I have never done before. Being inside her is my new hobby and I make sure she sees how much I like it.

Kammie

We go through the week looking after Tasha and having sex. It's a good week.

Tasha seems to be improving and she's hoping to go back to work next week, I think she needs to get out of the house. I go over to see her on Friday after she has been to the hospital, her mum is there so I know we will have a laugh. Of course they ask me about Luca, I don't tell them too much though, I want to keep it to myself for a while because I don't know where it is going myself. We watch films and giggle all day,

Tasha looks happy and I feel much better about all of this now that I've seen her like this myself.

I see Luca on Thursday night, he stays over but we don't have sex. What we have is about more than sex and even though I want to jump on him every 5 minutes, I know that we have something special, we spend the night talking about our childhoods and what we liked to do in our spare time. He even tried to convince me to join his gym, I'm not sure I can watch him flirting with other women though so I said I would join a different one.

"Why Kammie? Why won't you join my gym?" he's pouting.

I giggle and say "I don't want to watch women throwing themselves at you Luca."

"They don't throw themselves at me," I raise my eyebrows at him "Well maybe some of them do, but it's not like that honestly."

"It's fine Luca, I don't mind, I just don't want to watch it that's all." I don't know why I feel like that, I've never been the jealous type!

We talk about past relationships, well flings really and we laugh, more than I've laughed in a long time. It feels comfortable and I like it.

On Saturday night I go out with Jenny from work and meet Luca in Jesters. "Oh my god look at that cute guy checking you out" she says looking towards Luca.

"Watch this" I say to her walking over to him and kissing him really passionately. I turn around and walk back over to her and she is stood with her mouth open.

She smiles at me and then says "That's him isn't it?" She looks back over to Luca. "That can't be him, he's absolutely gorgeous."

I hit her on the arm "What do you mean? Are you trying to tell me that he's too good looking for me?" I start laughing at her as Luca comes over and pulls me into a hug and kisses me again.

He whispers in my ear "Are you having fun baby? Did you miss me?" I can feel his hands slowly moving down to the small of my back and pulling me in close.

I giggle and I hear him groan. "Luca can I introduce you to Jenny, she works with me. Jenny this is Luca!" They shake hands and Jenny starts laughing.

"You dirty mare keeping him to

yourself." Jenny goes to the bar to buy a round of drinks, Glen joins us and when she comes back from the bar we introduce them.

We have a great evening, lots of laughs, drinks and dancing. When I am on the dance floor Luca comes up behind me and starts gyrating behind me, it feels like foreplay to me. I'm going back to his house tonight and I can't wait, I am so turned on and can't wait to show him how much I want him later tonight.

When we leave Jesters it's about 3 in the morning and we walk to the coffee shop and have coffee and apple pie. Luca feeds me the pie as we laugh about our night out. When we have finished the pie we jump in a taxi and drive out to Luca's place, where I spend the night.

When we wake up in the morning, we lounge about in bed for a while just talking and making out. We go downstairs for breakfast at lunchtime and Luca starts to cook some food. He is such a good cook and I love watching him when he moves around the kitchen.

I text Tasha and tell her that I met Luca when I went out last night and we had a good night. I don't want to tell her that we are trying to have a relationship because I don't want to jinx what we have.

When I leave Luca's apartment later on the Sunday he drives me home. Just as I am getting to my house Felix rings me, that is really strange I didn't even think that he had my number, so I answer with a little trepidation "Hi Felix, is everything ok?"

I can see Luca looking at me as he pulls into my drive.

"Kammie have you seen Tasha today? She went out earlier and I haven't heard from her. I'm worried about her we had a bit of a row earlier." He sounds really upset.

"Felix I text her earlier and she replied so I am sure she is ok!" I wonder what has happened, he must be really worried to ring me.

"Thanks Kammie it's just not like her to walk out and ignore my calls, I'm sure she is fine."

"Make sure you tell her to let me know she is ok Felix, you've worried me now." I can feel myself start to panic, Luca has parked the car and has his hand on my leg, rubbing it to try and make me feel better.

"I will Kammie, I'm sure she's just pissed off with me." He says before he hangs up.

I don't say anything for a while and then Luca says "Is everything alright Kammie, you've gone as white as a sheet!"

"I think it is Luca, Kammie's walked out after a row and Felix can't get hold of her, he's worried about her and so am I now." I get out of the car and walk to my door.

Luca follows behind me and he puts his hand on the door to stop me going through it. "Baby I want to stay with you for a while, I can see that you're worried, let's have coffee and we can try and get hold of her."

I smile at him, he is always thinking about me and my feelings. "Come on then Luca" I say opening the front door and walking in. Luca goes into the kitchen and boils the kettle to make coffee and I turn the TV on, he brings the coffee into the lounge and sits next to me. I feel so comfortable with him being here, it scares me a little bit – but it makes me feel happy more than it scares me.

After about an hour or so I hear from Tasha and she tells me that she had argued with Felix and had walked to the park for a while to think things through. She says that everything is good and she was sorry that Felix had to ring me.

I curl up to Luca on the couch and tell

him what Tasha said. "That's good Kammie at least we know she is ok."

I can feel my eyes getting heavy and I know I am falling asleep. After a while I feel something move underneath me, it is Luca he is lifting me up and carrying me upstairs. "Luca" I slur the words because I am so tired.

"Baby you are knackered I'm going to put you to bed and then leave you to sleep" he says kissing me on the cheek. When we get to the bedroom he undresses me and pulls the covers up over me.

"Luca it's too early for bed, I won't sleep." I say as I turn and curl into a ball.

He leans down and kisses me on the cheek "Night night baby enjoy your sleep." He then starts to walk out the door and slowly closes it behind him. I fall asleep straight away.

19 Luca

A week later!

Who the hell is ringing me at this time of night? For gods sake it's 1o'clock, I pick the phone up and answer gruffly "yeah?"

"Luca, Luca it's me"

"What do you want Felix? It's the middle of the night" I know I sound angry and dammit I am angry.

"I'm sorry, I'm sorry Luca, I need you, I need you to come over and bring Kammie with you." Felix says, he's crying "Please before something really bad happens."

He's panicking and crying, what has he done this time? I swear to god if he's hurt Tasha again I'm going to personally kill him.

"Felix, what did you do? Tell me she's ok!" I'm getting angrier by the minute. I start getting dressed, I know he's going to need me to go to the house. He doesn't answer me, this is going to be bad I just know it!

"Felix, Felix talk to me NOW!" I'm shouting, I need him to talk to me.

"Luca, I've done it, I think I've killed her" he's sobbing. "What will I do? I want her, I need her, Luca, I need you mate."

This sounds bad, what the hell has gone on. "Felix I'm coming, I'm just leaving my house, I'll be there in 5 minutes, quicker if I can, stay on the phone and keep talking to me ok." I know I'm pleading but he sounds like he's slipping away from me.

"Felix, FELIX, what did you do?" I'm shouting.

"I think I killed her" he sobs.

"What did you do and why do you sound strange Felix?"

"I need help Luca, I can't be without her!"

I will remember that conversation as long as I live, I really thought he had killed

Tasha. That was the day that they both ended up in hospital. Tasha because of what Felix did to her – she had to endure surgery because of him. I don't know if I will ever forgive him.

He then tried to kill himself, he ended up in hospital and eventually he was put into psychiatric care. It is very hard to have sympathy for him when he hurt Tasha so badly, Kammie thinks that I shouldn't feel sorry for him. I've known Felix since we were at kindergarten and it's very hard just to switch those years off and not think of him. He needs me, other than his parents he doesn't have anyone, I can't desert him now, he needs me.

20 Luca

I know I've been spending too much time with Kammie, I haven't really stopped to think about Felix, he needs me, I need to tell Kammie that we need to slow down and that I need to concentrate on Felix for a while. It breaks my heart because I know I'm falling in love with her. Our love is so passionate and I find myself craving her more and more, the more I have her the more I need her.

She's been visiting Tasha and helping with her recuperation and I've been visiting Felix to make sure he is ok, I feel really guilty when I'm with her because I know that Felix needs me more right now than she does.

KRISSY V

I pick her up and bring her back to my place "Kammie we need to talk" jeez that's such a corny line even for me.

"What's the matter Luca?" she's looking at me with those beautiful eyes, I don't know if I can go through with it.

"Let's get a drink and then we can talk" she follows me into the kitchen where I pour her a drink, we take out glasses and go into the lounge and sit on the couch.

"Let me finish what I'm going to say ok baby, I need to say it and I want you to hear me out" she nods her head for me to go on, I can see the light going out behind her eyes, she's thinking the worst and she may just be right.

"What happened to Tasha was awful and Felix shouldn't be able to get away with it, I know she doesn't want to press charges, that's good of her, however, Felix has been my friend for years and I have to make sure he gets the care and treatment he needs." Again she nods but doesn't say a word. "So what I'm trying to say is that I need to spend time with Felix, he has to be my priority baby." She starts to open her mouth to speak and I hold my index finger up over her lips. "Please let me finish" I take a deep breath "I'm going to move in with Felix when he comes out of hospital, he needs me and I want to be there for him. I don't know what that means to us baby, I need you so much but I'm going to have to take some time out. If, when this is over and Felix is better, you still want to know me then it will make me very happy, if that takes too long and you move on then I'll just have to deal with that." I can feel tears coming to my eyes, I really need to man up.

I look up into her eyes and see she has tears overflowing "Baby please don't cry, it's not goodbye, it's just until Felix gets better. I know you want to be there for Tasha too." I lean forward and rub her tears away and kiss her on her eyes, she lets me that's a great sign.

"Why Luca? Why don't you think you'll have time for us? Is it too much like hard work for you?" There comes the anger, she stands up and starts pacing around the room. "I knew you wouldn't settle down, I knew you'd want to play the field sooner or later, well it's better it's sooner at least then my heart is only a little bit broken." She reaches down and takes a big gulp of her wine and then walks out of the room.

"Kammie that's not it at all, didn't you listen to what I just said, this is about Felix, and me helping my friend."

"He doesn't deserve your help Luca, you

are far too kind to him, he is a monster for what he did to Tasha. I know he's your best friend and I admire you for wanting to look after him, but don't expect me to wait around forever Luca, I can't promise that." She looks like she wants to burst into tears, I don't know what to do, I want to take it all back but I know I have to look after Felix, she has to understand that.

"Kammie please listen to me, you know how much you mean to me, it hurts for me to do this when all I want to do is keep you here all the time every day, but you need to look after Tasha and I need to look after Felix." I take a step towards her, she doesn't move, so I take a second step, then a third then I take her and pull her to me. I wrap my arms around her, lift her up so that she is straddling my waist and push her against the wall. I take her head in my two hands and kiss her as if I am taking my last breath, when I pull away I whisper "I hope you understand and know that I want to be with you and I will be with you again as soon as Felix is better, baby I need you to make me whole."

She returns the passion in my kiss and says "Don't take too long Luca, please." We kiss again and I can feel the emotion, when we break she has tears in her eyes and she slowly slides down my body. "I'm going to go home Luca, I need time to think about what you've said" and with that she walks over and takes her overnight bag and walks out my door.

I run to the door and shout "Kammie let me take you home, please" she just shakes her head.

"No I'll find my own way home I need to think" she walks up the road and around the corner.

I slam the door shut and I can feel myself getting mad "Why does Tasha and Felix have to fuck with this relationship again" I shout into the room.

I get into bed and lay on the bed thinking about Kammie and what she means to me and I realise that I'm falling in love with her and it doesn't scare me, what scares me is that I might have pushed her away and she won't come back.

I eventually fall asleep but have a very fitful night.

Kammie

I walk around the corner from Luca's house and I sit on a wall and cry, cry like my heart is breaking. This is why I don't do relationships!

It takes me about 15 minutes to compose myself and then I call a taxi and I sit and wait. I think about what Luca said and I know he's right, I know he needs to do this for Felix, I'd do the same for Tasha. I know she needs me right now, I've never been the sensible one but that is what I need to be right now. Why couldn't Luca be a bastard instead of a nice guy who is right? I get in the taxi and when I get home I shower and climb into bed.

When I wake up my head is hurting, I can feel a migraine coming on, it feels like an elephant is sat on my head and thumping his trunk against it. I roll over and pull the covers over my head. I lay there for a few minutes then I remember last night, I shouldn't have walked out on Luca, I should be adult enough to talk to him that's what he did with me. I want to ring him and apologise but I can't even lift my head, I fall back asleep thinking of Luca.

I wake up a couple of hours later and the banging in my head is really loud, hang on it's not hurting and then I realise it's someone banging on the front door.

"Kammie, Kammie open up" it sounds like Luca.

I roll over in the bed and go to the window, I open it and see him stood there, my heart misses a beat, he really is gorgeous. "Stop banging Luca, what do you want? I don't mean to sound mean but my migraine feels like a hangover."

"Kammie open up let me in please" he says looking up at me.

"Hang on it might take me a while to make it down the stairs just stop banging" I say then I slowly walk out of the room, I make it downstairs and I open the door.

Luca takes one look at me and takes me in his arms "Baby you look awful are you ok?"

"What are you doing here Luca?" it's all muffled because I'm still in his arms.

"Tasha rang me she wants to go and see Felix and asked were you going in to see her, she is going home today and I know you wanted to go with her. You wouldn't answer the phone so I had to come round."

"My phone is turned off because I have a migraine Luca, I feel like shit, although I feel better than I did earlier." Being in his arms is making me better but I don't tell him that. "Let me get a bag packed I'll stay with Tasha for a couple of days."

"Ok I'll make you a coffee while you get dressed and get packed", he kisses me on the head and then walks towards the kitchen. I go upstairs and sit on the bed, I really need to pull myself together. I don't want things to be awkward between me and Luca because then Tasha and Felix will be right! I get dressed and pack a bag then I go down stairs and take my coffee off Luca and lean up against the kitchen worktop.

We stand there looking at each other, I decide I have to say something "Luca I'm sorry I just walked out last night, I should have stayed and talked about it. It was immature of me, I was just shocked. I wasn't expecting it. I understand what you were saying and I know you're right, selfishly I wanted you to myself and I didn't want to share you with Felix. I'm sorry!" I look down at the floor fighting tears.

He reaches out and takes my free hand, he takes it to his mouth and kisses it "Kammie I was worried last night that you wouldn't talk to me again and that scared me a lot. I need you in my life and I thought I pushed you away. I'm just asking for a little bit of time to look after Felix, please. I'm not pushing you away I want this to work so bad."

He drops my hand and puts his finger under my chin and tilts it up gently, I love when he does that because he always gives me a big smile and I can feel him looking deep into my soul. He leans forward and my heart is beating like mad, he very gently kisses me on the lips and leaves his lips there. I want him to kiss me deeper, but I know that would make it harder for both of us.

We pull apart "come on then let's go find Tasha and Felix," he says picking my bag up and walking towards the door. I follow him out to the car, locking the door behind me. It's quiet when we are driving to the hospital, we both have so much on our minds.

"Luca, you'll let me know how Felix is doing won't you? I know Tasha will want to know. I want to know how you're doing as well because I know it's hard for you, I want to help you but I know you don't want help."

"Of course I will, I'll ring you later and let you know" he looks at me and smiles. "I'm hoping Felix is getting out in a couple of days so he can start to get better, I'm going to move in with him for the first week or two." I feel my heart drop as he says that, what will I do if I don't get to see him for a couple of weeks?

"Right, well we can talk and you can let me know how he is doing" I feel really sad, but I don't want to show it. I want to be strong for Tasha.

We arrive at the hospital and we go to Felix's room, Tasha is meeting me there because she wants to go to see Felix before she leaves. We stand outside with her dad while she goes in to see him. After a few minutes we hear a bit of shouting and Brian runs into the room and shouts at Felix. Tasha is crying and it is all a catastrophe.

I hug Luca, say goodbye and then walk out with Tasha and Brian.

21 Luca

When Kammie walks away I feel like my heart left with her. I really want her so bad, but I need to be there for Felix and by doing that I won't be able to give Kammie the attention she deserves. Once I give her my heart there's no going back, if we are meant to be together then everything will be fine once Felix is better. That's what I'm hoping for sure.

I take a deep breath and walk into Felix's room, he is raging mad when I get in there. He had told Tasha and Brian to leave so I told him that he can't treat them that way, that he owes Tasha an apology because of the way he treated her. He gets annoyed with me and tells me to leave, he says that he doesn't want me to move in with him. Today I saw a different side to Felix, this must have been what Tasha saw, it saddens me a lot.

When I drive home I know that I will be there for Felix tomorrow when I bring him home, so I pack a few belongings into a bag and put it in the back of the car, then I drive to Felix's house and make sure there are the essential items in the fridge and cupboards.

I spend the rest of the day and night tidying and cleaning up the mess that Felix made the other night. When I finally sit down I know that I want to talk to Kammie, so I ring her.

"Hey how are you all doing? How's Tasha?"

"Hey Luca she's ok, she a bit frustrated and doesn't understand it all but then again I think we all feel the same. How are you Luca? Are you bringing Felix home tomorrow?"

"I'm ok Kammie, I've just been cleaning Felix's mess up in the house, I can't believe the mess he made!"

"I know, but Luca you know I'm here whenever you need me, even if it is just to moan" she says and I know she means it.

"Thanks Kammie you really are an

amazing person."

"I know Luca, I know!" she starts giggling and right on cue my cock starts twitching in my trousers.

"Baby don't giggle like that please, you know what it does to me." This makes her giggle more, "I'm going to go and finish up here Kammie, you are just teasing me."

"I just don't want you to forget me Luca."

"That won't happen ever baby!" I hang up because now I have a raging hard on, I decide to go and take a cold shower because I know that relieving myself wont satisfy me, only being inside Kammie will do that.

When I go to bed that night I'm very unsettled, my life has changed so much in the last month and so much has happened. Who knows what the next few months will bring. I lay in bed thinking about Kammie, Felix and Tasha and I soon fall asleep because I feel mentally drained.

When I get up I get ready for bringing Felix home, then I go the hospital, his mum and dad are there when I get there. They are trying to convince him to go home to stay with them, but I know he won't do that.

Eventually they see that he wants to go home and nothing will change his mind, so they drop the subject and tell him they will see him over the weekend when he has had time to settle in.

Once he has been discharged, we get his belongings together and then I take him home. He is quiet on the way home, like he is thinking about something.

"Are you ok Felix?"

"Yeah I can't wait to see Tasha, why didn't she come to the hospital with you? I thought she would have." What is he talking about?

"Felix don't you remember yesterday she told you she wasn't moving back in! She's scared and doesn't trust you, you have a lot to prove to her before she will come back, if at all mate" he must remember, he needs to remember.

He doesn't answer and when we pull up to the house, he jumps out and runs to the door, when he opens it he walks in and starts shouting "Tasha, Tasha where are you" he looks frantic.

"Felix, she's not here, she's not coming back, not yet anyway." I say putting my hand on his shoulder.

He turns to look at me, he doesn't look like Felix, his face is red and his eyes are dark. "She has to come back Luca, she just has to. I'm going to find her and bring her back, she can't ever leave me!"

"Calm down Felix, calm down, you need to rest and you need to stay away from stressful situations."

"Get off me Luca and get out of my way" he says shrugging my hand off his shoulder. "I'm going over to Jean's house and dragging her back here. I need her, she's my wife! I think she forgets that sometimes, I need to show her she's still my wife!" He is really angry, if it wasn't because I was bigger than him I would find him intimidating, this is probably how he treated Tasha when none of us realised, it makes me sick.

"Felix stop right now!" I shout really loud into his face. "Tasha is not coming back, it's best for her to be away from you right now, you will get better quicker that way." He looks at me as if I've gone mad.

"Luca if you can't bring Tasha back home then you need to get out of my house" he is shouting at me and has so much hatred in his eyes. "I know you've always fancied your chances with her so go ahead, you've got what you wanted, she's a slut anyway."

I don't know what happened next but I punched him, he can't talk about Tasha that way, it's not right!

He's dazed, he obviously didn't expect me to behave like that. "You can't talk about Tasha that way, she was protecting you for so long because she didn't want anyone to think any differently about you, I am here to help you get better, even though I think what you did to Tasha was inexcusable." I have raised my voice too because I can't believe how he is behaving.

"I am completely aware of what I did to Tasha, don't you think I haven't gone through every minute of the last month or so in my mind. Every day I think about it and every day I feel so bad that I did that to her and ultimately pushed her away from me. I know that and I have to live with that day after day, but I don't need you preaching to me about what I did. I'm going to get better by being on my own and thinking about what I did. Luca I don't want you to stay here with me I want to be on my own."

"No way Felix you're not staying on your own, I want to help you, I want to be here for you when you need me, that's what friends do!"

"I know but I don't want that, I want to be on my own, so you can get your stuff and get out. I will be fine Luca, you can check on me if you want but I want to be on my own." With that he walks in to the kitchen to make a cup of coffee.

I stand there for a minute and then I go and pack my stuff up, when I come downstairs he is sat in the lounge with his coffee, he looks up and stares at me "Haven't you gone yet?" I can't believe how cold he is being.

"Felix you know where I am when you change your mind later." I say and walk out the door, I get in my car and drive home.
When I get into the house, I lay on my bed, thinking about Felix and how nasty he's being, I'm only trying to be a good friend and help him, yet his rejection hurts like hell.

I check on him over the next couple of days, he seems to be picking up. Maybe it was best to leave him on his own to cope, it seems to be the right solution.

22 Luca

I'm really angry that Felix won't let me look after him, but there is nothing I can do. I need to see Kammie, I've missed her this week so I ask her to come over for lunch. She comes over and I cook for her, it is so good to have her here, I realise how much I have missed her.

Me and Kammie are just relaxing after lunch when my phone goes, it's Tasha, I tell Kammie to be quiet so Tasha doesn't hear her.

"Hey Tasha" I say and there's no response, "Tasha..... Tasha ...." I look at Kammie who is starting to panic.

I hear some noise through the phone, then I hear a scream, then it goes quiet and then I can hear her saying "Felix stop, why are you doing this to me?"

"Tasha .. Tasha .." still no response then all of a sudden I hear "L...L...Luca. F...F...Felix" I can't believe this is happening again. "L...L...Luca. Ring Dad. Come quick, please" She's sobbing.

"Tasha, where are you? What is going on? I can't hear you very well, why are you whispering?"

"F...F...Felix, Luca come quick please. Home – I'm at home"

"Oh my God Tasha what has he done to you this time, I'll fucking kill him. Stay hidden and I'll be there as soon as I can. I'll ring your dad and ask him to meet me there. Love you Tasha."

My heart is beating really fast, if he's hurt her again I will personally kill him. "Kammie something's happened at Felix's, Tasha wants me to ring her dad, I'm going to head over, will you go to her mums I'm sure she will be worried. I'll ring you baby as soon as I know what's happened" I kiss her because she looks so frightened, all I want to do is protect her.

She starts crying "Ok Luca, promise me you won't do anything stupid, please."

"I promise baby, I promise" I hope I can keep that promise.

I drive over to Felix's like a lunatic, I hope I'm not too late, I hope he locked her in somewhere like last time to protect her. I see Tasha's dad's car in the drive and I jump out of the car and barge in the front door.

I see Brian cradling Tasha and I start looking around for Felix, she tells me he's upstairs, I walk to the bottom of the stairs and look up. "No no Felix no" I run up the stairs two at a time. I get to him "Felix why?" I feel for a pulse, there isn't one, I sink to my knees and start crying like a baby. Why did he do this? He has his whole life ahead of him. I wanted to help him and he wouldn't let me, it's my fault I should have just been there, I shouldn't have let him be on his own.

I hear Brian coming up the stairs behind me, "Luca I'm sorry, come on it's not your fault, he did this to himself. Tasha just told me that he asked her to come over, he told her you were going to be here, he set this up so that she would find him."

After the police have been and questioned us all we go back to Jean's house, it has been a very difficult day. I try not to blame myself, but if I am honest I do think that I could have prevented this.

Kammie tells me that I couldn't have and she pulls me into her and tries to help me forget what I saw today.

Out of all of this heartbreak, today is the day that I realise how much I love Kammie, I can't push her away any longer. We don't have a lot of time on this earth and it's not worth wasting it by being apart.

We all stay in Jean's house for the night, I sleep in the spare room and Kammie sleeps with Tasha. All I want is Kammie beside me in the bed, but I know she has to be there for Tasha, didn't I just say that only the other day about me needing to be there for Felix.

Kammie

When I see Tasha, Luca and Brian coming thought the door I throw myself at Luca, I know he doesn't want me right now, but he needs me.

He pulls me in so tight "I'm sorry Luca, I can't believe it, are you ok?"

He has his hands on the small of my back and one of them moves and entangles itself in my hair "I am now baby, I need you so much."

I can feel the tears that were desperate to fall "I'm here Luca, I'm not going anywhere, I need you too. I promise to look after you, I'll be here when you need me ok." I pull back and look into his eyes - they look so dull and sad, but I can a small glimmer of a sparkle and know that my Luca is in there, he just needs help to get out.

He smiles at me and we all walk into the kitchen where we get a stiff drink and toast Felix. We have a good night talking about the old Felix, no one mentions the last month or so, we don't need to.

When we go to bed, I want to hold Luca, I know he needs me tonight, but I know Tasha needs me more. She tells me to go to Luca, but I know that I'll be there tomorrow night and every night after that he needs me.

I wake up in the night and making sure Tasha is asleep, I creep out of her room into the spare room where Luca is. "Luca" I whisper, I know he hears me.

"Baby come here" he says, I walk over to his bed and climb inside. He pulls me close to him and wraps himself around me.

"Did I wake you Luca? I just wanted to make sure you were ok" he feels so lovely and warm wrapped all over me.

"I couldn't sleep, but I know I can now. Thanks baby for coming in to check on me. Thank you." I can hear his breathing start to slow down, his grip on me starts to loosen and I know he falling asleep. I roll slightly so that I'm on my back and he pulls me closer, even in his sleep he feels when I move. When I know he's fast asleep I kiss him gently on the lips and climb out of the bed.

I go to the door, open it and turnaround and look at him sleeping, he really is gorgeous. I can feel my heart leap when I think of him.

I go back to Tasha's room, go to the toilet and quietly climb back into the bed. I look at the ceiling and eventually fall asleep.

The next few days were hard for Tasha but also for Luca, he lost his best friend and he blames himself because he should have stayed with Felix and not left him at home. I tried to tell him that it wasn't his fault but he wouldn't listen. He's a stubborn guy, I keep talking to him about it even though he didn't want to. Talking is the best form of therapy.

Before the funeral me and Luca decided we were going to tidy Tasha's house because

Felix had trashed it, we didn't want her to know we were doing it. We were leaving Jean's house one day and we bumped into Caleb, the guy who had come to the hospital to see Tasha, he said that he would come over and help us. The day we went to tidy up he met us at the house and rolled his sleeves up and mucked in. He really is a nice guy, Luca got on well with him too. We needed to do some painting in the house and he made a call and someone called Dillon came to help us get it finished in time for the funeral. He is Caleb's best friend and we all had fun cleaning up the house.

After the funeral was a dark time for Luca, but I was there to help him and I think he realised that and let me in.

23 Kammie

Back to present day

Tasha and Caleb's wedding was so beautiful and everyone was so happy. Caleb cried when Tasha told him in front of everyone that she was pregnant. I can't wait to be an Aunty I am so excited.

The day after the wedding I wake up with a slight headache and roll over to look at Luca and I smile, looking at him always makes me smile. We moved in together about 7 months ago and it just felt so natural because we wanted to be together all the time, so it was silly to pay for his flat and my house. We sold his flat and he moved in with me. One of the first things we did was redecorate everything so that it felt like a new house and we had so much fun doing it.

Caleb has become Luca's best friend, he will never replace Felix, but he's the next best thing. Caleb's friend Dillon has been around quite a bit too and the three of them have such a laugh when they get together. Luca sometimes has nightmares about finding Felix and he will wake up in the night screaming, I'm always there to hold him and quieten him down. I think he got closure the same time Tasha did - when she read Felix's letter out to us all. We all jumped to the conclusion that Felix had rung Tasha to come over and find him hanging as his last bid to hurt her, that hurt Luca a lot because he never thought Felix would do something like that. When Tasha eventually read the letter and Felix explained that it was the only way to set her free, to stop him from hurting her anymore, that's when Luca was able to say goodbye. He regularly goes to the grave and sits down and talks to Felix, I know he misses him, but he is also moving on with his life too.

Caleb and Tasha are coming round for dinner tonight, they are going on their honeymoon tomorrow morning, so I said we would cook dinner, well Luca will. He is so good at cooking, I'll help him prepare and do what he asks me too but I will leave the cooking to him.

He wakes and sees me looking at him "Morning baby were you staring at me?" he smiles as he pulls me closer to him, I tip my head up to look at him and I nod my head. "Mmm I thought so, I could feel your eyes on me," he leans his head down towards mine and very gently kisses me on the lips.

Very quickly he turns me over so I'm on the bottom and he kisses me harder, "I need you right now Kammie" he says looking at me deep into my eyes. "I need to be inside you, the closest I can get to you, I need to know that you're mine and I have you."

He always gets deep and meaningful when Felix's memories are strong. "Luca I'm yours take me anyway you want" he kisses me with so much passion and I can feel myself getting turned on. I'm wet with anticipation of him being inside me.

All of a sudden he starts to move down my body, kissing me gently on his way down my body. When he kisses me like that every sense in my body is heightened, and each kiss feels like a mini electric shock. It feels good!

Luca

Caleb and Tasha arrive on time and they look so happy coming in hand in hand.

We hug them both and welcome them in.

"Thank you for a great day yesterday, Tasha you looked so beautiful" Kammie says.

"Thanks Kammie you didn't look too bad yourself, but it was a gorgeous day wasn't it?"

"Everyone was so happy, the weather was beautiful and there were some surprises for everyone too. How are you feeling by the way?" Kammie asks them both as we walk towards the dining area.

"I can't believe we are going to have a baby" Caleb says with the biggest grin on his face.

Tasha laughs "He is like a child in a sweet shop, he keeps asking me how I am, it is really going to annoy me by the end of the honeymoon." She looks at him and sees he is smiling.

"I have to look after my wife and child, that is a man's job!"

They sit at the dining table while

Kammie and I go out and bring the dinner in.

The food is delicious, we had fun cooking it because we were flirting the whole time. That's one of the things that I love about Kammie, the fact that she laughs so much, she is always happy.

Once we've eaten I make coffee for everyone and we sit around the table drinking it and chatting, everything is nice and relaxed and we don't have to think about what we say.

"How's work Luca?" Caleb asks genuinely interested.

"It's ok Caleb I enjoy my work but I just feel I'm slogging my guts out and not being rewarded for it. You know the usual complaints" I say laughing.

"Yeah that's why I work for myself, no one to bother me except myself and maybe Tasha" he says reaching across the table and taking her hand. I watch them looking into each other's eyes, they really do make a great couple, I've never seen Tasha as happy as she is when she is in the same room as Caleb. I don't think she was that happy with Felix, ever! I like Caleb, he's really down to earth and he is so easy to get on with.

"Yeah that's my dream too Caleb, just have to get that far in my plans" I look over to Kammie who is smiling at me, she takes my hand and nods her head, she knows what my plans are and she's behind me every step of the way and when we can get enough money together then I can open my own gym.

"Are you looking to open your own gym then Luca? I wasn't sure that's what you wanted to do." I can see his eyes start to sparkle.

"Yeah, I've even gone as far as writing my business plan, when I moved in with Kammie I sold my apartment and made a tidy profit. Even with putting some money away for savings and a rainy day, I'd have a good bit towards setting up."

Me and Kammie have talked about this and she is happy for me to use my money to fulfil my dream, eventually it would be our dream for her to leave her job and help with marketing, admin and all that office shit that I don't understand.

"Ok I can look at your business plan if you want to help you out, see where you want to take this idea and see how serious you are about it" Caleb says.

"Really, Caleb that would be amazing, I

didn't want to ask as you're so busy and with the wedding and honeymoon and everything, thanks." I reach across the table and shake his hand, I notice Tasha looking at him and smiling, I know it makes her happy when we get on.

"I tell you what lads, why don't you go and chat in the lounge, take your drinks, me and Tasha will clean up." Kammie smiles at both of us. She knows I appreciate Caleb's help.

We agree, stand up give them a kiss and walk into the lounge. We sit chatting and Caleb thinks that what I want to do with a gym is great and thinks that it would do really well.

"Luca you have some great ideas, the people you work for obviously don't know your potential, they will be sorry when you leave. I think it could do well. If you're prepared to hang on for 2 weeks until I get back from honeymoon with my wife" he stops and smiles for a second, "then if you want, come down to my office and we can look over your business plan. I can help you to tighten it up ready for when you go to a bank. Just don't do anything yet. Ok?"

"I won't be doing anything for a while, we need to save up some more money before that happens, so I'll be working where

I am for quite a while Caleb."

"Great Luca, I know this is going to be great for you, I might be able to help you with some contacts if you want."

"Thanks Caleb that would be great I wouldn't know where to start," we sit and chat for a while about gyms in general when the girls come in with their drinks, non-alcoholic for Tasha of course.

I'm delighted for her that's she's pregnant, I know Kammie is too. It makes me think about our relationship and where we are going. I know I don't want to be without Kammie, I'm not sure I'm ready to share her right now though. Saying that, if she got pregnant I wouldn't be upset. I sit and smile to myself. It goes quiet in the room and I focus on everyone and realise they are all looking at me, smiling at me. I smile back.

"What are you thinking about Luca? You had a funny smile on your face" Kammie asks.

I laugh "I was thinking about Tasha being pregnant and how that would affect our friendship and realised it wouldn't really affect it at all."

After a while Tasha says she needs to go

home, they are still living in the apartment during the week and the beach house at weekends, I think that will change when the baby comes along.

We walk them to the door and when we open it I wrap my arm around Kammie and pull her close. They say goodbye and we wish then a good honeymoon, they are going off to Bali and it sounds so idyllic.

When I close the door, I turn to look at Kammie and she smiles, I promised her that I would tie her up tonight, she loves that, so do I.

"Caleb seemed to be really interested in your gym ideas Luca, isn't that great!" she says turning and walking away. She knows I don't want small talk, she is teasing me, this is part of her game.

"Kammie get upstairs now I don't want to talk about Caleb" I say grabbing her hand, she slowly turns and looks at me.

"What if I don't want to" she says smiling mischievously. "What if I want to talk about Caleb?" she says smiling at me.

I don't wait to answer that question, I take 3 paces towards her, her eyes light up, she knows what is coming next. I see her turn to start running, but she's not quick enough. I reach out and lift her up and over my shoulder, she is hitting me on my back "Luca, Luca put me down" she can hardly talk she is laughing so much. I love when she laughs, she giggles and that turns me on even more. I put my hand up her dress until I can feel her ass, I can't feel any panties.

"Kammie are you naked under there?" It wouldn't surprise me, she doesn't wear panties when she is at home, but with us having guests I thought she might have some on.

"Yes I am, am I naughty?" she giggles.

"Kammie, I need to get you up these stairs stop giggling!"

24 Kammie

Luca has me over his shoulder, I am hitting him on his back until he runs his hand under my dress to reveal that I'm not wearing any panties. He is almost running up the stairs, he can't get to the top of them quick enough. I love it when he gets all manly and commanding, it really turns me on. He kicks the bedroom door open so hard it bounces off the chest of drawers, we really must get one of those door buffers. He takes about 3 paces to reach our bed and throws me down. I can't stop laughing, I find it funny when he gets all alpha male on me because he is such a pussy cat.

"Kammie, stop laughing" he growls, he pulls me so I am sitting up in the bed then in one swift movement he pulls my dress up over my head and throws it across the room.

He stops and takes a step back to look at me, "You really are so beautiful do you know that" he smiles at me while he slowly undoes his belt and pulls it out of his trousers. I know what is coming next and I can't wait.

He undoes his buttons on his fly, one by one, as slowly as he can. All the time he is watching me and my reaction with every button he undoes. Then he takes his trousers down and I see that he has no underwear on either. "Luca I think you've been naughty too!" I giggle again. I see his eyes open wide as he walks over to his bedside cabinet and goes straight to the bottom drawer, my eyes open wide because I know what he keeps in that drawer. He looks at me and then looks back into the drawer, like he is trying to decide what to pull out of it. "Come on Luca, I'm feeling lonely here!" I giggle.

He smiles and then he pulls out the black silk ties, I like them, they feel soft around my wrists and ankles. He crawls back up and onto the bed and then he silently takes one of my wrists and pulls it closer to the bed post and wraps the tie around my wrist and then around the post. He repeats what he did with the second wrist, then the two legs. When he's finished he stands up and looks at his creation, he smiles and then the fun begins.

He tortuously kisses every inch of my body, from my toes up to my eyes and then works his way back down again. I squirm underneath him and start giggling as he kisses my nipples and then he takes one of them in his mouth, his mouth feels really hot on my erect nipple. He flicks it with his tongue and I can feel the pressure building inside of me.

I try to move away from his tongue, it is driving me crazy, he tilts his head up to look at me and he smiles with my nipple in his mouth. He starts to groan and the vibration goes through the whole of my body. He lifts his head and moves over to the other nipple and repeats it all again.

"Luca, please move it's driving me crazy, please" he giggles and that only makes it worse.

"Kammie I need you to not lose control, this is going to be slow and beautiful" he smiles as he starts to kiss slowly down my stomach to my belly button. He runs his tongue inside my belly button and I start giggling, it always makes me laugh.

"Luca stop, stop" he doesn't, he keeps running his tongue around the rim and then plunging it into my belly button.

He laughs and says "I'll stop" and then

he moves further down until he reaches my lips, once again he lifts his eyes to watch my face, to see my reaction. He kisses them gently and then starts to push his tongue in between them and then he licks very slowly. I moan, he is really driving me crazy tonight.

"Kammie, control it baby" he continues licking me and then he pushes a finger inside me. I moan some more. He takes his finger out and plunges two inside, I start to squirm it feels so nice. "Baby you taste so good, I want more" he takes his finger out and slowly pushes his tongue inside. It feels so good, and then he starts to wiggle it inside me. He is driving me crazy tonight!

"Luca I can't hold on much longer I need you inside me, please" he lifts his head and smiles at me.

"You taste so good but I know you are going to feel much better when I'm inside you." He moves his body to an upright position, he leans over and takes the ties off my ankles, he rubs them for a minute until I have some circulation back.

He starts to crawl back up my body and then he hovers above me with his large, bulging cock lined up at my entrance. "Is this what you want Kammie? Tell me what you want! Tell me how much you want it!"

He pushes the head of his cock so that it is just inside my lips and then he hold his body up by leaning on his hands. He stops, waiting for me to speak. "Luca, please"

"Baby you know what I want so just tell me" he says and I hear how much he is turned on too.

"Luca I want you inside me and I want you to fuck me hard."

"Manners Kammie!"

"Please Luca I want you to fuck me hard" I shout because I really want to push him in but my hands are still tied to the bed.

He grins and then tortuously slowly pushes his cock inside, when he is all the way in he stops. He needs time to control himself, I can tell he is really turned on and just wants to fuck me, but I know he wants to go slow tonight.

He starts to move in and out "Is this what you want Kammie?" he says as he continues to move slowly.

"No Luca I want you to fuck me HARD." I am really shouting now, he needs to understand that I want him to ram his cock in and out and make me sore tomorrow.

He smiles at me and then he starts to move faster and harder, he slams his cock inside me and I groan every time he does because it hurts when he does, but in a good way. I slowly move my feet so that they are wrapped around him and I try to push his ass so that his cock goes in deeper. "Kammie what are you doing?" Oh dear he might tie my legs up if I keep this up, I don't care, I want to push his ass and if I have no arms to do it then my feet will have to do!

I smile at him, he knows what I am doing. "Please Luca let me cum."

He smiles back at me and he reaches over and takes a pillow and wedges it under my ass to lift me up, he then reaches for each leg in turn and puts them over his shoulders. Now I am really lifted off the bed, I watch him in puzzlement, when all of a sudden he rams his cock inside me.

"Oh my god Luca, oh my god" it hurts but it feels so good, I know it won't be long before I cum.

"Baby that feels so good, I'm so deep inside you right now, this is what I want forever, I want you forever Kammie. We were made for each other, we fit perfectly, we both know what we want." He keeps ramming his cock inside me and then it's too much for me.

I feel like I am on the top of a rollercoaster looking over the edge, I know what's going to come and I am waiting for it, then I fall over the edge and it is a bumpy ride, but it is exhilarating. I feel my muscles start to clench and tighten over his cock while I cum all over it.

"Kammie oh my god, that feels so good, I can't hold on any longer sorry baby" he says as I can feel his cock growing inside me and then he pumps his hot cum into me. He continues to move very slowly in and out until he is spent, then he slowly lays himself down on top of me kissing me passionately. "That was amazing Kammie, I love you so much, nothing will ever make me as happy as being with you."

"I love you too Luca, with all my heart" and then he lays down on top of me panting. After a couple of minutes he pulls himself out of me and rolls over onto his side and pulls me close so he can kiss me on my neck.

"Luca did you forget something?" I ask looking at my hands.

He laughs "looks like I did" he leans over and takes the ties off my hands, he rubs them until I get my circulation back. "Come here baby and get into my favourite position." I roll over so that I am facing away from him and then he pulls me in tight. This is where I belong!

Epilogue

Kammie

Everything is perfect! Tasha and Caleb came back from their honeymoon with amazing news. We all met up for dinner and Tasha told Luca that she was giving him Felix's share from the sale of the house. She said that she doesn't need it and Felix would want him to have it, Luca helped her and Felix a lot when things were really bad and she believes that he deserves it. Luca, of course, didn't want to take it, but after much discussion and persuasion he agreed that he would use the money for opening his gym.

Caleb, Luca and Dillon have been spending a lot of time going over the business plan and Caleb asked Luca did he want to put a gym into one of his residential properties – the one where he lives. If that goes well, then Luca will open more in the other premises.

I've been spending time with Tasha, getting ready for the baby arriving. Meg has been joining us and she is becoming a very good friend too.

Luca

These last few months have been a rollercoaster of emotions and I am finally going to be living my dream of opening my own gym, and if this goes well then who knows how many I can open. I wouldn't have been able to do this without my friends, but mostly without Kammie. She has been my rock, she is the reason I get out of bed every morning and she has driven me to fulfil my dream.

I can't wait for the gym to get established, then Kammie is going to come and work alongside me and we will truly be partners in life.

Who would have thought that two players could find such happiness and fulfilment together?

The End!

Acknowledgements

As usual I have had a lot of help from a lot of people. My pimpers, beta readers – I love you all! I have had new members join my team and I want to welcome them all on my rollercoaster ride.

I have had help with some of my technology from my good friend, Rebekah Spiller, so much so she has called herself my "Social Media Manager". Xx

I couldn't do this journey without you, my readers, you are the reason I am still writing books.

About the Author

You know who I am at this stage, so I won't bore you again!

I hope you have enjoyed Luca and Kammie's story and look out for the last book in the Til Death Us Do Part:

Dillon and Meg's story – For Richer or For Poorer

This will be released in the next couple of months so watch out for it.

After the Til Death Us Do Part series is finished, I have another couple of books which are currently "Work In Progress" so stay tuned to my website: authorkrissyv.wordpress.com for further details.

I love to hear what my readers have to say about my work so please find my links below:

Facebook:
https://www.facebook.com/authorkrissy.vas
Goodreads:
https://www.goodreads.com/author/show/8039636.Krissy_V

Thank you for your support and I hope you have enjoyed this series of books as much as I have enjoyed writing them.

Krissy V

Made in the USA
Charleston, SC
28 June 2014